Mo Wren
LOST
and
Found

Tricia Springstubb

BALZER + BRAY
An Imprint of HarperCollins*Publishers*

Also by Tricia Springstubb

WHAT HAPPENED ON FOX STREET

Balzer + Bray is an imprint of HarperCollins Publishers.

Mo Wren, Lost and Found
Text copyright © 2011 by Tricia Springstubb
Illustrations copyright © 2011 by Heather Ross

Library of Congress Cataloging-in-Publication Data
Springstubb, Tricia.
Mo Wren, lost and found / by Tricia Springstubb. — 1st ed.
        p.   cm.
Summary: After living her entire life on Fox Street, eleven-year-
old Mo Wren must adjust to her new life—living in an apartment
on East 213th Street, above the "cursed" Corky's Tavern.
ISBN 978-0-06-199039-7 (trade bdg.)
    [1. Moving, Household—Fiction.   2. Family life—Fiction.
3. Restaurants—Fiction.   4. Neighborhoods—Fiction.]   I. Title.
PZ7.S76847Mm   2011   2011001896
[Fic]—dc22   CIP
                                                                   AC

Typography by Sarah Hoy
11 12 13 14 15   LP/RRDB   10 9 8 7 6 5 4 3 2 1
❖
First Edition

For that wild and wonderful little sister, Jessie

Mo No Go

4 SALE BY OWNER, said the sign.

At first the words had shouted, but by now they just sort of muttered. Since last summer, the sign had gotten drenched by rain and beaten up by wind. For Halloween, one of the Baggott boys festooned it with toilet paper, and at Thanksgiving an early snowstorm topped it with a sparkly white cap. Around Christmas the weather warmed up, setting Fox Street melting and dripping. In the Wrens' muddy front yard, the faded 4 SALE sign tilted sideways. You could almost hear it saying, "Really, I've tried my best, but I'm getting tired out here."

That New Year's Day, Mo Wren was the first one up. She pulled on her jacket and stepped out into the bright morning. Not a soul in sight. Being a dead end, Fox Street was naturally more peaceful than most places. But this morning's hush was different. Mo told herself everyone was worn out, after staying up late banging pots to chase the old year out and being serenaded by Baggott firecrackers, not to mention the *whoop-whoop* of the patrol car when old Mrs. Steinbott had called the police on them. Up on the corner, the Tip Top Club had celebrated big-time. Fox Street, Mo told herself, was just sleeping in, gathering its mojo for the new year to come.

A sparrow flew down and perched above the 4. Cocking its brown head, it fixed Mo with a questioning eye.

"Happy new year," she said, and to her own surprise the words came out in a whisper, as if the morning were a sleeping dog she'd better not disturb.

A car turned the corner onto the little street. For the most part, nobody came down Fox Street unless they lived here or had made a wrong turn. Since the 4 SALE sign had gone up, though, a number of prospective buyers had found their way to the Wrens' door. They stood in the yard to peer up at the roof and trooped down to the basement to inspect the pipes. After a while they let loose with a low whistle, mumbled thanks a lot, climbed back into their cars, and took off without a backward glance.

Each time, Mo's breath whooshed out in a grateful sigh of relief.

The car made its slow, clanky way down the street. In the front seat, two swiveling heads checked out the houses.

"Uh-oh," she whispered to the sparrow. "They're looking for us."

Mo didn't want anyone buying their house. She didn't want to move away. Oh, what a measly sentence that was! Like saying a bird would rather not fall out of the nest, or a fish disliked the idea of getting hooked from the river.

Since Fox Street was so short, only five houses on each side, and since the Wrens' house stood right in the middle, the car didn't have far to go. It stopped with an extra-loud clank, as if it had just made it. And then the hush returned, but not all the way. The morning had a hole poked in it now. Something was going to happen.

The car doors opened. With an alarmed *cheep*, the sparrow took off.

Mo watched a young man and woman climb out. The man shaded his eyes in the bright sun, gazing at the Wrens' house, while the woman leaned into the backseat and brought out a baby. The baby had a pink hat and eyes like raisins. As her mother carried her toward the house, she pointed a chubby finger at Mo.

"Go!" she commanded.

"I live here," said Mo.

"Well, you're a lucky one, then," said the father. "This looks like the perfect street to grow up on!"

"It is," said Mo before she could think. "I mean, it's all right."

The man's name was Tim. His wife was Sarah, and the baby was Min.

"I'm Mo."

"Go!" yelled the baby.

"No, Mo. Mo no go."

The baby stared, and then a laugh popped out of her, like a cork from a bottle. Her parents both laughed too.

"She likes it here already, don't you, Min?" Sarah had dimples in both cheeks. "Have you lived here long?" she asked Mo.

"Eleven years. My whole life. I was born here."

"My goodness," said Sarah, but before she could add anything more, Mr. Wren hurried out the front door, stuffing his shirt tail into his pants.

"Happy new year!" His curly hair was uncombed, and you could see the pillow crease in his cheek. He shook hands all around, even with Min.

"I bet Mo's been telling you what a great neighborhood this is. She and her little sister love it here. Love it! It's kid heaven. A cul-de-sac with a Metropark at the end of the street? And you couldn't ask for better neighbors. We hate to go, but things change. Come on, I'll show you inside."

Cul-de-sac! Where'd he get that? The family followed Mr. Wren into the house. Min had pulled off her hat, and her black hair shone like a little helmet. Mo guessed she was adopted from China. Imagine traveling thousands and thousands of miles, across all those countries and continents, all the way to Fox Street. To this very house. It was amazing. Almost an honor.

What was Mo thinking! Who said they'd buy the house? She pulled in a lungful of sun-warmed air. Fox Street was waking up. In his driveway Mr. Duong popped the hood of his car and peered at the engine. The Baggotts' front door flew open, and Baby Baggott ran outside naked. Hands over head, he did a few laps around the yard but must have gotten cold, and he ran back in. Next door, Mrs. Steinbott swept her spotless porch, waved to Mo, and went back in.

"Happy new year, Mo!" Pi Baggott rolled by on his skateboard. Glancing back to make sure Mo was watching, he flew across the pothole in the middle of the street. Mo's heart skipped, as if she rode on the board too.

Her whole life. More than a decade. Every person she truly cared about was from Fox Street.

Including her mother. She was still here, even if she wasn't.

Mo resolved to ignore the morning's strange foreboding. She was a thinker, after all. So, *think*. Why should Min's family be any different from the others who'd looked at the house? Judging by their car, they weren't exactly rolling in money. It was obvious—that 4 SALE sign wouldn't be coming down anytime soon. In fact, it was time to straighten it up. Mo yanked it out of the ground and was preparing to set it squarely back when the front door opened again and her father jumped down the steps.

"Whoa!" he cried. "Let's not count our chickens. But I bet you're right. I think this is it."

"It?" Mo clutched the sign like a shield.

"They're up in your room—Sarah says it's the perfect little-girl room." He smiled. "They both keep saying everything's perfect. Of all the people who've looked at the place, they give me the right feeling."

"But . . ."

"They're not just looking at a house, Mo. They're already seeing a home." Mr. Wren took the sign and leaned it against the porch rail. "Cross your fingers," he said, and dashed back inside.

Mo crossed her fingers. But she knew her wish and her father's didn't match.

Origami Life

For most of her life, Mo had understood next to nothing about adults. But one thing she was sure of: They were in charge.

So if her teacher was mean and unfair, Mo assumed the woman chose to be like that. If a neighbor was grouchy, or a sales clerk scolded, "Hands off the merchandise, kid," Mo figured they enjoyed pushing other people around. When her father grumbled over his job, or kicked the lawn mower instead of trying to fix it, or sat at the kitchen table with his head in his hands, Mo would think, He could be happy if he really wanted to.

Grown-ups were in charge of everything else. They must be in charge of their feelings and their actions. Right?

But the older you got, the more complicated life was. It began to resemble origami, where what you see is a crane or a rabbit, but not the dozens of folds and creases that went into creating it. Mr. Wren *did* want to be happy. He wanted them all to be happy—him and Mo and Dottie, the way they used to be years ago, before the accident. He wanted this with all his might, like a bodybuilder struggling to raise weights off the floor. But no matter how much he grunted and strained, he couldn't do it. Not since she had died.

For Mo's mother, being happy had been as easy as flowing is for water. And like water, her happiness needed to spread, so anyone who came near her got swept up too. Mo remembered her father, who'd never met a job he liked, coming home from work. The minute he stepped through the door, his crabbiness vanished, like a bear's pelt falling away to reveal a prince. One arm went around her mother and the other scooped up Mo. Sometimes the three of them put on a dance party right there in the kitchen. Other evenings they'd lie beneath the plum tree, counting the fruit like purple stars.

Dottie came along later, for better or for worse. While Mo had dark hair like their father's, Dottie's head was covered with wild red curls like their mother's. Mo could remember being out in the backyard, supervising her baby sister as she picked up fallen plums and plopped them in a bucket. All at once she'd hear her father singing. Having a terrible voice didn't stop him. When he was happy, he belted out a tune. And when he was home, he was happy.

It could have gone on like that forever! Happy and safe and simple. But three years ago, a furniture truck came speeding down Paradise Avenue just as Mrs. Wren stepped off the curb. Bystanders said the truck came out of nowhere, and that was where it left Mo, Dottie, and Mr. Wren.

Since she'd died, Mr. Wren's happiness had dwindled down to a sliver as thin and transparent as the last lick of a lollipop. The lines between his dark eyes just dug in deeper and deeper. Sometimes, when he and Mo strolled down the street, a woman passing by would give him a second glance. You could almost hear her wondering, "What would it take to cheer that broody man up?"

As time went by, Mr. Wren hatched his own cheer-up plan. Sell their house on Fox Street and use the money to buy a new place. He'd always dreamed of being his own boss, and what could be better than a neighborhood sports bar? Mr. Wren knew how to grill a mean burger, and he loved to talk sports, especially baseball. It'd be a family place, where parents took their kids after the school concert and teenagers could crowd into a booth and eat cheese fries after the game. Breakfast—Mo's favorite meal—would always be on the menu.

Mo got uneasy hearing about it. For her, happiness was digging in, watering your roots. For her father, it was more along the lines of jumping off a cliff. But the daydream made her father happy, and who doesn't want to see her father happy?

Things had taken a turn last summer, when he'd found a tavern for sale across the river. It was in a neighborhood full of potential, Mr. Wren said. When Mo asked what that was supposed to mean, he said the new neighborhood was part of the future, not the past. Corky's Tavern had been empty for months, and the price was right. A new coat of paint, some elbow grease—they'd turn that place right around. Upstairs was a nice cozy apartment—think of it. He could work and live in the same place. They'd always be together!

He even had a name for the restaurant. The Wren House.

If only he could scrape together the money for a down payment!

Whack. The 4 SALE sign went into the ground.

And then the months crept by. Months when the lines in his face made Mo think of origami creases that never smoothed out. Months when she wished with all her might for her father to be happy, and wished just as hard that they'd never have to leave Fox Street. Two opposite wishes that, maybe, canceled each other out. Because there the sign still stood. And here the Wrens still lived.

Until the morning of New Year's Day.

The Brave

"Give me strength," said Mo's neighbor, Da Walcott. Leaning on her cane, she ran her sharp eye over the piles of stuff on the Wrens' tree lawn. "I wish I could help. This is a big job, Mo Wren."

Mo swallowed. Every time she turned around, the thought of something else she was going to miss hit her square in the chest.

1) the plum tree
2) Mrs. Steinbott's roses
3) the ravine (also known as the Green Kingdom)
4) Pi Baggott (this being a secret)

Now she'd have to add

5) the funny way Da makes my name sound like
   Moron, not on purpose, of course

"Our new apartment's not that big," Mo said. "And besides, a lot of this is just junk."

As if to prove her right, along came Leo Baggott and picked up a broken toaster.

"Only one side works and you have to hold it down the whole time," Mo told him. "Plus sometimes it gives you a shock."

"We're used to eating our bread raw," he said, tucking it under his arm with satisfaction.

"One person's trash is another person's treasure." Da wrapped her scarf tighter around her swanlike neck. The cold weather was back, a few snowflakes drifting down. "So who bought the house in the end?"

"It was weird. These people with the baby and the clunker car? Sarah and Tim? They came to see it, and then the next day another couple did too. They both wanted to buy it. All of a sudden, our house turned popular."

"Those people with the fancy eyeglasses?" said

Da. "Snazzy little red car?"

"Umm-hmm. She's an architect—it sounds like knocking down walls is her specialty. He wants to have his law office here."

Da, a retired schoolteacher, pressed her lips together as if waiting for a student to stop hemming and hawing and get to the answer.

"So," said Mo, "they had what you call a bidding war. But it was over pretty soon."

"Well, money talks." Da frowned and fingered the edges of her scarf. "I bet that poor young couple was heartbroken."

"Oh, no. Daddy sold to them."

"He did!" Da looked astonished. "Well. Your father's never been the predictable kind."

Mo nudged a broken-bottomed doll stroller with the toe of her shoe. It didn't matter to her who bought their house. What mattered was that she had to leave it, and soon. Just that morning, her father had quit his job at the water department. One of the trash bags held his muddy uniform. It was like he couldn't wait to put every last bit of their old life behind them.

"It's natural to feel upset." Da possessed a teacher's mind-reading ability. But it was more than that between the two of them. Da had known her all her life. Even before, she liked to say, since she and Mo's mother had been fond friends. Not only that. Da was grandmother to Mo's best friend, Mercedes, who came up from Cincinnati every summer to stay with her. In eleven years, Mo had spent nearly as much time in the Walcott house as she had in her own.

"You love Fox Street better than anybody," Da said. "This isn't going to be easy for you, child."

Da gave a shiver. She had diabetes, and last winter she'd had four of her toes amputated, a polite way of saying "cut off leaving nothing but stumps." She wasn't supposed to be outside long, her circulation was so bad.

"Have you talked to Mercey about moving?"

"Not really," said Mo. The truth was, she and Mercedes didn't talk much when they were apart. For Mo, her friend's school-year life had a hazy quality, like the view through a smudged window. And yet the minute Mercedes showed up, the very June morning they were reunited each year, it was as if they'd never been separated.

Mo squinted through the thickening snow at Da's house. She could almost see Mercedes and herself sitting on that front porch, drinking Da's puckery lemonade, the long summer days stretching out before them. Da said she and Mo's mother used to relax on that same porch, in those same chairs with the backs like seashells, listening to the ball game on the radio.

Mo swallowed again. She wondered if she was going to have this lump in her throat for the rest of her life.

"That's probably because she's still in shock," said Da. She waved her cane at a black bird pecking one of the trash bags. "After a decade as an only child, I guess that's natural."

"What? I mean, excuse me?"

"Monette's due in June." Da leaned on her cane and smiled. "Princess Mercedes is going to be a big sister. That poor child is already bitten with the mad dog's tooth, jealousy. So you see, Mo Wren, you're not the only one whose life is undergoing considerable upheaval."

Mercedes a big sister! One more thing they'd have in common.

"You know they're forever pestering me to move down there." Da's smile faded. "Now there's going to be a baby, they have more ammunition. Monette says she needs my help, but they don't fool me. I'm the one they're worried about. Give me strength! If I moved down there, they'd fuss me to death!"

"Da! Are you going to move away too?"

"I said no such thing." Da thumped her cane. "If there's one thing I prize, it's my independence! Neither a borrower nor a lender be!"

A gust of wind blew down the street. An ancient spelling test lifted from the pile and twirled like a giant snowflake. Da shivered again.

"You should go inside," Mo said.

"'Come inside, Da.' 'Rest yourself, Da.' ' Did you do your physical therapy, Da?' 'Should you be eating that, Da?' Night and day!"

She gave a ferocious scowl, then turned on her heel. But one of her orthopedic shoes skidded on the ice, and she lurched sideways. Mo grabbed her arm.

"I'll walk you back," Mo said.

Da looked about to protest but changed her mind. Arm in arm, they crossed the street to the foot of Da's front steps. The branches of the ancient lilac were growing fat with snow.

"Never forget, Mo Wren," she said, gripping the railing. "True hope is swift, and flies with swallow's wings!"

Swallow—what a bad name for a bird! Mo trudged back toward her own house. The wind blew into her face, making her eyes tear up.

Inventions

Mo and Mr. Wren shoved things into the rented moving van, then pulled them out, then piled them back a different way. No matter what configuration they tried, some things refused to fit.

A corner of their big green armchair jutted out into the winter day. "How about we leave Min and company the chair?" asked Mr. Wren.

Mo spread her arms to protect it. It was called a wing chair, for the way the sides curved around you like the wings of a fuzzy mother bird.

"Look," he said, poking his finger into the cushion. "It's got that hole."

"So? We can fix it!"

Mr. Wren sighed. "This is what I get for promising to bring everything you want. Short of hitching the whole house to the back of this truck . . ."

"Dottie's beer bottles! Where are they going to fit?"

"Beer. That's the most inspired idea I've heard all day."

Their footsteps sounded loud in the front hall. Empty of their things, the rooms were big and blank. The walls looked embarrassed, as if caught without clothes on. Mr. Wren trudged into the kitchen, and Mo pounded up the stairs.

Dottie was still packing her bottle collection. She laid each one in the box with great tenderness, giving it a reassuring pat.

"Don't be afraid, Rihanna. Oh, Brad, we're going on a great adventure—you'll like that. Guess what, Boopsie? Our new apartment has a shelf just waiting for your cute little self!"

Though it was freezing outside, she wore her usual outfit: a gigantic T-shirt and nothing else. Dottie never got cold. She was like a walking six-year-old space heater.

"Did you hear?" she asked Mo. "When we move, I'm getting a pet."

"Daddy said?"

"Probably a monkey."

"You're a monkey." Mo picked up a green bottle and wrapped it in newspaper. When her little sister's forehead wrinkled, she knew what was coming.

"Mo?"

"Yes. When we move, you'll still be my sister. There's no way around it. How many times do I have to tell you?"

Dottie took the bottle and nestled it in with the others. "I heard Daddy tell Mrs. Petrone this is his big chance to reinvent himself." Dottie dug her knuckles into her cheek, a thing she did to keep from sucking her thumb. "So I started thinking, if he gets reinvented, he'll be somebody else, right? Like a stranger. And then I thought what if you . . ."

"Mo!" their father shouted up the stairs. "Run up to Abdul's and get us some sandwiches!"

"In a second!" Mo licked her thumb and wiped a smudge from her sister's fuzzy apricot of a cheek. "You know what?" she told Dottie. "You're thinking too much. Leave that to me. I'll always be your big sister, and Daddy will always be your father."

"Mommy quit being our mother."

Mo grabbed another bottle and wrapped newspaper

around it once, twice, three times. Nothing short of a bomb was going to hurt that bottle. She got to her feet.

"Your bottles are going on a big adventure, and so . . . so are we."

Back downstairs, Mo got money from her father and stepped outside. She stood still for a moment, waiting for the cold to clear her head. Dottie's little brain was still so muddled. Mo tried to remember being like that but had the feeling she'd always been more grown-up than Dottie, and of course always would be. How on earth could a person get reinvented? That meant you had to be invented in the first place. Mo zipped her jacket up. Things got invented. Telephones, elevators, internal combustion engines. Not people. Not Mo. She just *was*.

By now the street was deep in afternoon shadows. Soon people would be coming home from work. It'd be dog-walking, mail-fetching, dinner-shopping time, and Mo sped up, determined to be back inside before then. She'd been doing her best to avoid saying a last good-bye to people. Or bad-bye, as Dottie called it.

But uh-oh. Oh, no. Here came Pi Baggott, sailing toward her on his skateboard. Tall and princely, he might have been riding a magic carpet. Over and over he'd offered to lend her his board and teach her to skate. But going fast, not to mention defying gravity, did not appeal to Mo.

It might have been nice to take a lesson or two, though. Pi would have been a good teacher. Now it was too late.

"Mo!" His breath was a silver cloud. His shaggy hair lifted in the breeze.

Pretending not to hear, she broke into a run.

Travelers

In the yellow kitchen, her father was sound asleep in one of the chairs that wouldn't fit in the van.

Mo set the bag of sandwiches on the floor and tiptoed past him, out the side door, careful to catch it before it banged. Her father had always meant to fix that door. Outside, night wove the day with dark ribbons. Mo crossed the little backyard to stand beside the plum tree. Mo and this tree had known each other so long, its trunk and her spine were best friends.

The moon was rising. Wherever you go, Mo's mother used to say, the moon comes too. The moon got to travel. But not a tree. From now on, Min was the one who'd play beneath the plum tree, and gather its fruit in a bucket, and settle herself against it whenever she got sad or lonesome. If the tree minded, if it missed Mo, too bad.

Mo rested her cheek against its smooth bark. Already this felt like one of the longest days of her life.

"I've got to go soon," she whispered. "But I have one of your pits packed in my suitcase. If we really stay there, I'm going to plant it."

She felt jealous of that tree, and sorry for it, both at the same time. Confusion like this was a bad sign, for a thinker. Mo gave the tree one last hug. She walked down the driveway, fingers trailing the side of Mrs. Steinbott's house. The beautiful rosebushes were mummified in burlap. Out on the sidewalk, Mo matched her feet to the stripe of moonlight. No one was out, and she was grateful.

She passed Mrs. Petrone's house, and Ms. Hugg's, and came to the dented rail that guarded the end of the street. Beyond it, the land sloped steeply, a tangle of trees and brush tumbling down into the Metropark she called the Green Kingdom. By now it was too dark to see much, but she stood there listening to the rustle of a plastic bag caught in a branch. Once, once

Mo had spied a fox down there. The fox of Fox Street. Remembering how thick and lush that red fur was, Mo knew her fox wasn't cold, even tonight.

You just never knew how many things you loved until you had to say good-bye to them. It was amazing and terrible, both at once.

"Good-bye," she whispered. To the trees. To the stream below. To the secret hideout she and Mercedes had made. To her fox and to all the animals nestling in and burrowing down as darkness wrapped around them. "I'll never forget you."

"Me neither."

"Aargh!" Mo staggered backward. "What are you doing here?"

"I knew you'd come down here sooner or later," said Pi.

"You've been lying in ambush?"

"It's public property."

Pi was as unlike the rest of his troublemaking family as a candle from a wildfire. Talking to him had always been an easy, satisfying thing.

"Where's your skateboard?" she asked. You never saw him without it. But Pi just shrugged.

"I guess you're going," he said.

"I guess so."

"Yeah." His hands dangled at his sides. His toe nudged a broken piece of asphalt.

"Maybe you can visit when the Wren House opens. I bet my dad would give you a free burger and fries."

"It's not gonna be the same," he said.

"That's not what you're supposed to say!" Mo kicked away the bit of asphalt. "You're supposed to tell me how when one thing ends, something new begins! Wish me luck, then tell me I don't need it. Don't you know the rules?"

Pi jammed his hands into his pockets. His newest road rash, a scrape on his cheek, shone in the moonlight.

"I guess not," he said.

"Great. Thanks for nothing, Pisces Baggott. That was so helpful."

Mo whirled around and marched toward her house.

"It's dark," he called after her.

"Oh, really?" she yelled.

"You should wait till tomorrow."

How she wished! But there was her father, wide-awake now, waving to her from the driveway.

"Mo! Where've you been? Come on."

Out of nowhere all the rest of the Baggotts appeared, a whole stampede of them. Leo Baggott pushed Dottie in a cart stolen from the E-Z Dollar.

"It's time, Mo!" she yelled. "Daddy's coming back for the rest of the stuff tomorrow. We're going to sleep on the air mattresses tonight! Come on! We're going! Adios, amigos!"

As if she was Paul Revere, people began pouring out of their houses. Mrs. Petrone had to give them one more box of her pizzelles. Mr. Duong had another toaster, one he'd fixed up good as new. Ms. Hugg skittered down the street in her pink high heels to plant big smooches on their cheeks. As Mo passed her house, Mrs. Steinbott came down her steps carrying a crinkly knit bag.

"Look inside, dearie!"

When Mo loosened the drawstring, spicy-sweet perfume floated up and out on the cold air. Dried rose petals, scarlet and cream and pink, sifted between her fingers, turning the world upside down, making summer bloom even as the snow started up again.

"I'll miss you," Mrs. Steinbott said. "Watching you grow up has been one of my life's joys. I hope that new little girl's half as sweet as you."

"We better get out of here," Mr. Wren said, climbing into the truck. He wiped his eyes. "Before I make a fool of myself."

Dottie scrambled up beside him, but Mo held back. She was turned inside out, the most tender parts of herself open to the air. She couldn't leave. She just couldn't.

"Give me strength!"

Across the street, Da was coming down her front steps. No coat, her face twisted in a scowl.

"It takes forever to get these odious shoes on! I almost missed saying good-bye to my girl!"

There were people who hugged, and then there was Da. But now, as soon as Mo was in range, Da pulled her close. Mo could feel her heart beating like a tiny bird trapped under her ribs.

"I'm depending on you to tell me what moving on is like." Da looked into Mo's eyes. "You're a truthful, sensible girl. You'll be my advance scout."

"Okay, Da."

"I expect detailed reports," Da said into her ear. "It's called doing reconnaissance."

"Oh, Da."

"Remember." Da gripped her by the shoulders. "Every cloud engenders not a storm."

"Okay."

"And whom does fortune favor?"

"The brave."

"Go on, then. Go forth, Mo Wren."

As Mo crossed the street, Dottie stuck her head out the truck window and waved.

"You look both ways when you cross streets!" Da called to her. "And silent sustained reading, at least twenty minutes a day."

Dottie blew kisses. The little Baggotts threw snowballs. Where was Pi? Vanished. Mr. Wren tapped the horn. What could Mo do? The time had come.

She climbed in beside her father and sister.

"Fasten your seat belts," she told them.

And they were off.

WILCUM!

East 213th.

Their new street didn't even have a name. Just a number.

That was only the beginning of how different it was.

For Mo, Fox Street was such a slouchy, comfortable, lived-in place that walking along it was like thumbing through her own closet, looking at clothes she'd worn over and over, knew inside and out.

But East 213th was a confusing street, with a discombobulated, mishmash feel to it. Buildings lined both sides. The bottom floors were businesses, and up above were apartments. Every few feet, you came to a door—doors to the shops, doors to the rooms above. Lots of windows, too. Turn the corner and you could look in on a man getting a beard trim, kids picking out doughnuts at the Pit Stop, or a woman chewing a pen and frowning at a computer. In the windows above, a white cat, or an old man leaning his elbow on a pillow, might watch you go by.

None of them knew Mo. And Mo didn't know them.

There was more.

Fox Street was so settled in its ways that if somebody decided to plant a new shrub or paint his porch, everybody offered advice. But this neighborhood had a restless feel, like a snake continually needing to shed its skin. Several street-level windows were soaped over, with big COMING SOON signs. An old shoe store had turned into a coffee shop so quickly, customers drank their lattes sitting in rows of trying-on chairs.

And not only that.

Being a dead end, where Fox Street began and where it stopped were perfectly clear. *Once Upon a Time* and *The End*. But if East 213th was a story, it'd say *To be continued* . . . with those three dots that meant anything might happen. In one direction the street stretched two blocks before it ended in the park, and in the other, well. After three days, Mo still hadn't come to the end. It could stretch to Pennsylvania, for all she knew.

Eastside Park was the neighborhood's name. But Mr. Wren preferred Land of Opportunity.

"For once in my life, I'm in the right place at the right time," he told Mo as he cooked them burgers in their restaurant's industrial kitchen.

There was a jumbo stove with burners like big steel spiders. A fry-o-lator and a walk-in refrigerator. An enormous blackened vent. In one corner sat a box full of ancient potatoes, resembling shrunken heads. Fly strips, dotted with little black carcasses, dangled from the ceiling.

Corky, the former owner, had closed up one night and vanished. Well, not completely. His apron, streaked with what Mo hoped was old ketchup, still hung from a hook on the wall. According to the bank that'd sold it to Mr. Wren, he'd also left behind an avalanche of unpaid bills.

"Poor guy didn't have a clue what he was doing," Mr. Wren said. "Hate to say it, but his gain's our loss."

"We know what we're doing, right?" said Dottie. She lay on her stomach, busily crayoning. "And that reminds me. When are we going to the pet store?"

"I'll tell you where you're going," said Mr. Wren,

"and that's your new school. I registered you both today."

Dottie rolled onto her back, paddling her hands and feet in the air like a bug in its death throes. Neither she nor Mo was much for school. Dottie hated rules, and Mo was a slow worker, terrible at finishing things on time. But at least at their old school, all the teachers knew Mo. Every report card she ever got praised her for her diligence and hard work.

"Could you wash this Wild Child's hair tonight?" Mr. Wren asked Mo. "And lay out some appropriate school clothes?" He fixed Dottie with a stern look. "Underwear. Underwear will be required."

Back home on Fox Street, upstairs and down were two halves of a whole. But here, an invisible line divided private from public. Corky's had once been a regular old house, but someone had knocked out a wall here, and added a big plate glass window there, and *ta da*, the downstairs was reinvented as a business. Mo and Dottie crossed the empty dining room to a narrow back hall, where the restrooms were. Behind a door marked PRIVATE, steps led up to their apartment.

This apartment was small, as Mr. Wren had promised, and, with all their old furniture crammed in, resembled an obstacle course. Their green armchair took up most of the hallway. The cushion had torn a little more during the move, and a plume of white stuffing puffed out.

Mo's bedroom faced the street. She could see the row of buildings opposite and a big mound of snow on the corner. A skinny tree grew out of a square of dirt beside the sidewalk. Its branches swooped upward, like a figure skater at the end of her routine. Some genius had painted Mo's window shut. The sounds of East 213th bumped against the glass, trying to get in—the rumble of a bus, the slam of a car door, the shouts of some boys on bikes, out way too late for a school night.

What were the Baggotts doing now? And Da? And . . .

"Tuck me in, mochacho," said Dottie.

You wouldn't think you'd be able to get to sleep in a place so different, with so much on your mind. But somehow, the next thing you knew, your father was waking you up, and you were looking at a strange wall stamped with the shadow of a skinny tree. Somehow it was the first day at a new school, something you hadn't experienced since you were five years old, and your stomach was way too uneasy for you to eat, and you were running late, and your little sister made you later still because she insisted on stopping to tape to the front window the sign she'd made with her crayons.

WILCUM WRENS!!!!

And it was no use informing her *other* people were supposed to do the welcoming. You were out on the busy morning street, in the Land of Opportunity, where everybody had somewhere to go, and nobody paid a bit of attention to you, never mind stopped to say welcome.

The Curse

"Guess what time it is in Beijing," said a voice at Mo's elbow.

It was recess, and she hovered on the edge of the school playground. Across the street, Eastside Park sparkled like a snowy oasis. The morning had lasted a century or two, what with the new rules she had to learn, and being too slow to complete her timed diagnostic math test, and a girl at the lunch table who took one look at Mo's can of Tahitian Treat and said how terrible sugary drinks were for you. Mo had been looking forward to recess, but now she stood here all alone and freezing. Well, not alone.

"Guess!"

Mo turned around. A bony wrist wearing a watch with all kinds of complicated dials was inches from her face. The wrist belonged to Shawn, her classmate. All morning, she'd watched him drive teachers cuckoo.

"I don't know," she said.

"Guess!" Short and wiry, with skin the color of walnut shells, Shawn was one of those boys who had to be in motion at all times. Even when he was supposedly being quiet, he gave off a little hum. Now he jittered his wrist at her.

"I don't like guessing," said Mo.

"Midnight."

He grabbed the fence and rattled it, something Mo had resisted doing.

"It's tomorrow in Australia," he said.

"Does that watch also tell you how much longer we have to stay out here?" she asked. "Because I'm turning into a Popsicle."

"Are you from Florida or something? Sometimes it gets so cold here, ice cubes come out of your mouth instead of words. People have to take the ice cubes home and melt them to have a conversation."

"Ha ha. For your information, I moved from

the other side of town."

Shawn grinned, his braces glinting. He gave the fence a halfhearted kick. "Well, welcome to prison. Want to know a secret?"

"Like what?"

"Like Mr. Grimm asked me to be your bud."

Mr. Grimm was their math and science teacher. Mo already had doubts about the man, and this confirmed them. First of all, didn't he notice that Shawn was a boy and Mo wasn't? Second, didn't he know that all that stuff about opposites attracting was wrong?

Of course, it was possible Shawn was making this buddy business up. So far, Mo didn't have much reason to trust him, either.

"So," he said, "if you have any questions, just ask. I'm here to help. By the way, where do you live?"

"We bought this place called Corky's."

"Corky's?" Shawn's eyes went round "You moved into *Corky's*?"

"Why? What's wrong with that?"

"Sorry to break it to you," said Shawn, "but that place is under a curse."

Mo felt a prickle at the nape of her neck. The recess bell rang, and all the frozen-toed, teeth-chattering kids ran to line up. But Mo caught the sleeve of Shawn's jacket.

"What are you talking about?"

"Bad stuff happens to anyone who lives there. Nobody, repeat nobody, lasts for long."

"You tell whoppers," she said. "I don't believe you."

"You don't have to. Just ask around."

When school let out, Mo hurried to Dottie's classroom to pick her up. Crowds of kids passed by, ignoring her, making her feel like a rock in a rushing stream. She pretended to examine the zipper on her backpack, and to be extremely interested in the cutout snowflakes on the bulletin board. At last Dottie appeared, holding hands with a girl barely bigger than a fire hydrant.

"Bye, Diamond," she said. "Make sure you look both ways when you cross the street."

"That was Diamond," she told Mo as they stood beside the crossing guard. "She's in kindergarten and I'm her first-grade buddy and also I'm the E.S.P. That stands for Extra Special Person because Ms. Thomas said that's the best way for everyone to get to know me, so I got to feed the hamster and I gave him a teensy bit too much, but Ms. Thomas said that was an honest mistake and . . ."

"Wait." Mo came to a halt. "You like school? Is that what I am hearing?"

"Like!" said Dottie. "It's the best school I ever been to. This cute girl named K.C. says she always wanted red hair just like mine. And at lunch we have this club called the Cone of Silence with these secret signals, like if you wink two times that means do you want to trade sandwiches. And . . ."

By now they were walking across the park. On a bench, two old men huddled deep in their jackets, throwing popcorn to the pigeons. The swings cradled nothing but mounds of snow. High in a tree, the tail of a stuck kite rippled in the wind.

On the edge of the park stood a little bus shelter. Two of its three sides were see-through, but the back wall was solid white. Or it had been, before a million people scribbled on it. Some of the writing was impossible to read, and some was words Mo didn't like Dottie seeing. But a lot of it was who loved who. Alejandro loved Baby, and Louisa loved Mikey. Chris loved Kelly. Also Jess and Olivia.

The shelter was empty, and a bus rolled by without stopping. All of a sudden, Mo got that lump in her throat. Poor shelter, standing on the corner so faithfully, doing its duty day in and day out. People just

41

passed through or used it for autographs. They never gave it a second thought.

"Mo?" Dottie tugged on her hand. "What's the matter?"

I'm feeling sorry for a bus shelter. Mo swallowed around that stupid throat lump.

"I . . . I didn't have such a good first day as you, that's all."

No sooner had they turned onto East 213th than Dottie began to run. A narrow alleyway, inhabited by big trash cans, separated Corky's from the building next door. Al's Shoe Repair belonged to a short man with big, hair-spurting ears. He was behind the counter, examining a red high heel. The shop's shelves held flat tins of polish, loops of shoelace, pairs of shoes wrapped up and tagged. Mo had always liked the idea of fixing a thing rather than throwing it out. She waved to their new neighbor. In return, he gave her a curt nod, then turned away.

Did he know about the Corky curse? Was he afraid it was contagious?

Dottie was already in their house, perched on a stool, watching herself munch chips in the big mirror behind the bar. Mr. Wren was taping something to the dingy green wall. As Mo slid off her backpack, her hunched-up shoulders eased down for the first time all day.

"The Dot rocked her day," Mr. Wren said. "How about you?"

"It was okay." Mo slipped off her jacket. "What are you doing, Daddy?"

"What color should we paint?" He pointed to the rainbow-colored strips he'd stuck to the wall. "Meadow Sweet? Lively Lime? How about, geesh, Serious Violet?"

Dottie spun her stool. "Yellow," she said. "That was Mommy's favorite color."

Mr. Wren turned around. He pinched the bridge of his nose.

"The way I remember," he said slowly, "she was an equal opportunity color person. She loved them all."

"Silly Daddy." Dottie spun harder. "Just ask Mo."

"Hey, Dizzy Dean." He stopped the stool and lifted Dottie off it.

All of a sudden Mo had to sit down, ambushed by a memory.

The yellow sweater.

The Yellow Sweater

When Mo was small, her mother came home from the store with a new sweater. It was pale yellow, the color of the moon when it first peeks over the rooftops. Its buttons made Mo think of the moon, too—round and pearly. Her mother bought it on discount, the way she did most of her clothes, and afterward laughed at herself for buying something much too big.

But one day when Mo climbed onto her mother's lap, the two of them had made a great discovery: The sweater was so roomy, it could wrap around them both. Tucked inside, Mo and her mother had their own private moonbeam house.

"Now I know why I bought it," her mother said.

When her mother died, Mo never thought to ask her father to save that yellow sweater. Back then, she just assumed it would always be there for her, like the stars in the sky, or the plum tree.

By the time she got around to asking him where it was, Mr. Wren had looked startled.

"Oh," he'd said. "I gave all her clothes away, right off. Looking at them made me want to die myself." He'd touched Mo's cheek. "I thought you knew that."

"No. I didn't."

"I took it all to a nice charity. The ladies there promised me her things would go to people who'd really appreciate it."

For weeks after that, Mo was on the lookout out for an appreciative woman in a baggy yellow sweater. It was like being a detective, on the watch for stolen property. Not that Mr. Wren had stolen her mother's things, exactly.

Still, Mo had been sure that if she spied someone wearing the sweater, and explained, that other woman would whip it right off and return it to Mo, who was, anyone would agree, its rightful owner.

Little by little she'd given up looking. She hadn't even thought about that sweater in a while. Not till now, when her father held out the fistful of paint strips, like a papery bouquet. Mo spread them on the bar, considering. One, Buttercup Morning, looked very close to the color of their Fox Street kitchen. But something tugged her hand toward a paler shade, one shot through with silvery light.

Holding it up, she remembered all the times she'd climbed inside that sweater. Sometimes because she was sad, sometimes because she was happy, sometimes just because. Her mother let her sit inside as long as she wanted, till at last she was ready to ease herself back out. Then her mother would bend down and kiss the top of her head.

And the magical thing was, all the rest of the day Mo still felt that sweater wrapped around her. Like the moon, following her wherever she went.

Now Mo turned the paint swatch over to see what it was called.

Moonglow.

"This one," she told her father.

"You got it." He kissed the top of her head.

For the first time since they'd moved here, Mo felt truly happy.

That didn't last long.

Uh-Oh

They kept running out of Band-Aids, even though they bought the giant economy-size packs. Every day Mr. Wren got nicked or burned, bruised or scraped. Back on Fox Street, he hadn't been much for handy-man work. Their back door had been broken since forever, and Mo, in her heart of hearts, had thought it was because her father was lazy. But now she had to wonder if he really was just bad at fixing things.

"Maybe you should hire a helper," she said, the afternoon she came home from school to find him missing part of his left eyebrow. He wouldn't talk about how that happened.

"I'm doing just fine." He stepped to the big front window and frowned at the falling sleet. "There's no rush. The dead of winter isn't a good time to open anyway."

They'd bought the Moonglow paint. But no sooner did they start preparing the walls than chunks of plaster fell out. That meant spackling, waiting for it to dry, then sanding. Now the walls were an atlas of dingy green seas spotted with bright white islands. And the floor was grimier than ever.

"I'm just saying." Mo did a little jig. The furnace had something wrong with it, too, and she could never get warm enough. "Some of these jobs might go quicker if we used a . . . you know. An expert."

"We're doing fine, Mo." Still he kept his back to her. Mo could see his bald spot, a little clearing in that forest of black curls. "Just leave it to me. The two steps forward and one step back—that's the dance we're doing."

His voice was edging toward "that's the end of this discussion." Just then a can of creamed corn slowly rolled out from behind the bar. The dining room floor sloped, and little by little the can picked up momentum till *whomp*. It hit Mr. Wren's foot.

"Score!" Dottie poked her head out from behind

the bar. She was barefoot, in short sleeves. As usual, her personal thermostat was set on high.

"Very funny," said Mo. Her sister's happiness was getting on her nerves. Dottie hadn't even unpacked her beer bottles yet. The box, labeled TREJER, sat on the floor of her room, forgotten. She was like a little train that had switched tracks and chugged right on.

Mr. Wren picked up the can of corn and tossed it from hand to hand. Mo knew he considered the conversation over, but something made her press on.

"I mean, it's good to be thrifty and everything. But we got buckets of money from selling the house, so . . ."

"Let's get something straight." Mr. Wren set the can down with a thump. "This isn't our old life."

"I know *that*."

"Your job is to make new friends, and work hard in school, and look out for each other." He folded his arms and rocked back on his heels. "In other words, to be normal, growing girls." He came down flat on his feet. "The rest you leave to me."

"I'm just trying to help!" Her father's words stung Mo. "You always say what good ideas I have! I thought we were going to be partners!"

Another can rolled across the floor. This time,

when Mr. Wren stooped to pick it up, Mo saw him wince. His hand flew to the small of his back.

"This is your chance, too, Mo. You should be having a life of your own, not just hanging around here. Leave the worrying to me. *Not*," he added, "that I'm worried."

"But . . ."

"I applied for a small-business loan, and once that comes in, we're set. Nothing but blue skies."

"Then I can get a pet," said Dottie. She jumped up, bent her knees, and pretended to stir a giant pot. "The dance of joy! Wait till I tell K.C.!"

"K.C., K.C! That's all you care about!" Mo grabbed Dottie's arm and dug her fingers into it. "Can't you stop being so selfish for one minute?"

"Ow! Owie ow ow!"

"Don't you pick on your sister!" Mr. Wren thundered. "She's making a good adjustment. You could learn a thing or two from her."

Mo drew back her hand as if she'd gotten bitten. Her father hardly ever yelled at her, and he never compared her to her little sister. Dottie stuck out her tongue, then ran out of the room. Frowning, Mr. Wren turned back to the window. The sleet fell at a sharp slant, making all the world look as off-kilter as the floor beneath their feet. Al the shoe-repair man hurried by. He kept his eyes straight ahead, as if the Wren House was invisible.

"I repeat," Mr. Wren said. "From now on, nothing but blue skies for the Wrens."

Icy sleet walloped the window.

The Soap Opera

"What are you looking for, Mo?" Dottie asked.

"My red sweatshirt. The nice faded one, my favorite? I haven't seen it since we moved."

By now they'd run out of clean clothes. There was a washer in the basement, but when Mo turned the switch, it growled like a giant with a bone stuck in his throat. A stink of burning rubber poured out.

"There's a Laundromat on 215th," Mr. Wren said. "I'll drop you off and swing back around after my errands."

"Where you going, Daddy?"

"The hardware store, where else? That chick who

runs it says I'm financing her vacation to Mexico. Then the bank, to see what's holding up that loan." He settled his baseball cap on his head, dark curls sproinging out around the edges. "And then if I've got time, a restaurant supply place, to price glasses."

The windows of the Soap Opera Laundromat were all steamed up. Inside, the place was packed, as if everyone in the neighborhood had run out of towels at once. Washers chugged and driers thumped. An old couple folded sheets together, stepping close and then apart as if doing a dance they knew by heart. The big plush bench, once the backseat of a van, and all the plastic lawn chairs were occupied. A girl in a college sweatshirt worked on a laptop. A woman with platinum blond hair and earrings like crystal chandeliers cradled a pile of paper, talking to herself. By the door, a man who looked as if he hadn't used the Soap Opera's services in quite some time moved his lips while reading the newspaper.

Only one washer stood empty. As Mo and Dottie stuffed everything into it, a hand came to rest on Mo's shoulder.

"That will never do," said a deep, throaty voice. "Even on heavy soil, you'll never get all that clean."

She'd have been the queen, if Laundromats had

them. Small and dark skinned, she had hair that fell in luxurious dreads, and her hollow cheeks were dusted with something that glinted in the overhead lights.

"But there aren't any other washers," said Mo.

"Number Four only has three more minutes on it." She extended a royal hand. "Carmella."

"Mo."

Her wide smile showed crooked, unqueenly teeth. She helped Mo buy a swipe card and showed Dottie how to set for presoak. Then, carrying the rest of their clothes, she led the way to Number Four.

"Yo, Mo!"

It was Shawn, waving an enormous pair of men's boxer shorts like a flag.

"There's someone tickled to see you," said Carmella.

"He's in my class," she said. "His name is—"

"Oh, I know Shawn. His mama and I are old friends. He comes here most afternoons, and now and then he helps with fluff 'n' fold." She turned and called to the woman with the chandelier earrings, "Gilda! Your clothes are ready, girl! Oh, Homer, you leaving us? Hold on."

She dug into a bin in the corner. After a moment

she pulled out a fuzzy blue scarf and wrapped it around the neck of the man who'd been reading by the door. "It's cold out there," she said, buttoning up his coat.

Homer smiled as if he knew what was coming. "How cold, Carmella?"

"Why, it's so cold that when you open your mouth, ice cubes pop out. It's so cold that this morning, my shadow froze to the side of a building and I had to leave it behind!"

"Hah," Mo said to Shawn. "Now I know where you get your whoppers. You steal them from her!"

Gilda pulled a lacy heap of underwear from Number Four, and Mo loaded the rest of the Wren laundry. Soapy scents sailed through the air. The TV on the wall was tuned to a cooking show, where a woman demonstrated how to make coconut chiffon cake. Mo watched Shawn fold a pile of baby clothes, rolling pastel socks into cottony Easter eggs. Never had she seen him so calm and focused.

"You're good at that," said Mo.

"I'm good at lots of stuff! You should see me run. I'm so fast it takes three people to spot me. One to say here he comes, one to say here he is, and one . . ."

". . . to say there he goes!" Carmella chimed in.

"Enough tall talk, mister."

She fitted a key into the door of the vending machine and swung it open. At the sight of row upon row of junk food there for the taking, Dottie gasped. She gazed at Carmella the way primitive man did at fire. Carmella winked.

"Take your pick, Red."

When Dottie had her Skittles, Shawn his chips, and Mo her peanut butter cups, Carmella locked the machine back up. She folded her slender arms and watched with pleasure as they tore into their treats.

"Where do you two girls stay?" she asked.

"Corky's," Dottie told her. "My daddy's doing an expensive revolution."

Carmella's eyebrows disappeared into her hair.

"She means extensive renovation," Mo said.

"My guess is it's expensive too." Carmella shook her head. "Corky's. My my my. I wonder where that sorry man is now. "

"I told Mo all about the curse," Shawn said.

"Curse?" Dottie froze, something she never did with sugar in her hand.

"There's no such thing." Carmella gave Dottie's shoulder a squeeze. "Besides, every curse was made to be broken. Will you look at that—your clothes are almost done! Let's find you a dryer."

Once their wet clothes were tumbling, Carmella went back to work.

"Bedtime in Madagascar," Shawn said, displaying his wrist with its big, complicated watch. "Breakfast in Alaska."

"So is Carmella your auntie or something?" Dottie asked.

"She's my mom's friend. I used to go to the library till my mom got off work. But it's too noisy there. I'd rather hang here."

"I wonder if I could get a job here," said Dottie, eyeing the vending machine.

"You've got enough chores to do at home," Mo informed her. "You didn't even unpack all your stuff yet!"

"I wouldn't bother unpacking. Considering the curse." Shawn knocked his fist against his forehead and cut his eyes toward Dottie. "I mean. That is. If there was such a thing. As a curse."

"You can't scare me," said Dottie. But she inched closer to Mo.

"What makes you sure something bad happened to Corky?" Mo harvested a bit of lint from Dottie's hair. "All we know is he vanished in the night."

"You ever hear of somebody vanishing in the night for a good reason?"

Pins and needles prickled Mo's skin. She jumped up to check their clothes, just as Mr. Wren poked his head in the front door and waved.

"I'm double-parked!" he yelled, and ran back outside.

Shawn helped Mo and Dottie toss their clothes into the basket. As they hurried for the door, Carmella called to wait. Reaching into the bin in the corner, she pulled out a book and handed it to Dottie. *Caring for Your Pet Lizard.*

"I got a baby doll in there, too, but you're not doll people, I can tell."

"Ooh," said Dottie. "I love reptiles."

What *was* that bin, anyway? Like a magician with a hat, every time Carmella reached inside, she came up with a surprising and perfect thing.

"Don't let your laundry pile up like that again, you hear?" Carmella pulled open the door and clucked her tongue. "That your daddy? The man looks like he's about to take a bite out of the steering wheel?"

Mo shoved the basket into the backseat, and she and Dottie squeezed in beside it. Both the front seat and the floor beneath their feet were piled with boxes labeled THIS SIDE UP and FRAGILE.

"You got beer mugs!" said Mo, examining the pictures on the sides. "And water glasses!"

"That supply place had some great deals." Mr. Wren squinted into the side mirror. "The trunk's full, too."

"You got a lot done!"

"Yeah, well. The bank didn't take near as long as I expected." All at once he stepped on the gas and shot out into traffic, making someone behind them blast the horn. "Your momma wears a mustache!" Mr. Wren yelled.

"Did you get the loan okay?" Mo asked.

"You see all the stuff I bought?" he said.

Clean clothes perfumed the car. Dottie read aloud the many reasons lizards make ideal pets.

"They are not messy or nosy."

"Noisy."

"They can be very in—"

"—telligent."

Mo studied the back of her father's head. Had his bald spot gotten bigger since this morning? That must be scientifically impossible. Probably she was just viewing it from a different angle, since his shoulders were hunched so close to his ears.

"Lizards don't get lonely," Dottie read, and turned

a puzzled face to Mo. "How can that be?"

Their father shot through a light as it turned red, setting off another round of honking.

"Your momma sold her car for gas money!"

The Pits

"Mo!" cried her best friend. "Is it really you? I was just thinking of you, and the phone rang. You're a mind reader."

"I knew you were going to say that."

Mercedes laughed. Mo sank into the green armchair wedged into their upstairs hall.

"I'm going bonkers," Mercedes said. "The baby's a devouring monster! It's not even born, and it already took over. Half the time my mother's throwing up and the other half she's cooking disgusting, inedible food. Last night she put cinnamon in the mashed potatoes. Normally her intelligence is way above average, like

61

all Walcotts'. But the blood must be going to her belly instead of her brain. She cries over everything, at the same time saying how happy she is."

Mo drew her knees up to her chin and listened to Mercedes describe how nervous her stepfather, Three-C, was about the baby, his first, and how he followed her mother, Monette, around with sweaters and cups of stinky herbal tea that only annoyed her, since she was always too hot. Yesterday Monette had bought something called a breast pump, which Mercedes was too freaked out to even ask what *that* was.

Mo poked her finger in and out of the hole in the armchair upholstery, waiting for her turn to talk. When Mercedes paused for breath, she grabbed her chance.

"It's so strange," Mo said. "I can't picture where you are. And now I'm someplace you've never been, either."

"What? Oh, cripes—I almost forgot! You moved!"

"You forgot?" Mo sat up straighter.

"I mean . . . I always think of you on Fox Street. Sometimes when I can't fall asleep because I miss Da, or Three-C made me furious, I picture you there, and I don't know. It's like counting sheep or listening to a lullaby. I feel so safe." Mercedes's voice dipped low.

"But whoa. You're not there."

Mo pulled a tuft of stuffing from the chair. All of a sudden she felt like she was nowhere at all. Like she and Mercedes were nothing but sound waves vibrating on the thin, cold air. She gripped the phone as if it was trying to get away.

"Merce?"

"I'm listening."

Mo had so many things she'd planned to tell—about her unfriendly new school, and what a little traitor Dottie was, and how the more her father lectured not to worry, the more she did, the way you try not to pick at a scab but your fingers just keep going there. Before she could decide where to begin, Mercedes spoke again, the words coming out in a rush.

"Da had to go into the hospital for a couple of days because her sugar got so out of whack."

"What? She did? Oh, no."

"And the gutters leaked inside her wall, and before she knew it, part of the dining-room ceiling fell in."

"Oh, no!"

"Not on her! But still. She's having a really bad winter. "

"If I was there, I'd help her. I'd go over every day." Looking down, Mo discovered a little pile of chair stuffing in her lap. She tried to poke it back in.

"It's not right for her to be alone. Monette keeps begging her to move down here, but you know Da. Now she says she's waiting for reports from some scout." Mercedes's voice sank, weighted down with worry. "Do you think she could be going, you know, demented? Like old people do?"

Mo got to her feet, not an easy operation, since the armchair hogged almost all the floor space.

"Da? Never!" What could she say to cheer her best friend up? The pits! That was it!

"Merce, when you feel really bad, take your pit out and look at it."

"My what?"

"You remember! Last summer I gave you a pit from my plum tree? And we swore that if I ever moved, we'd plant them in our separate yards, on the very same day, at the exact same moment, so they'd grow up to be twins?"

"Oh. Yeah. Those pits."

"It's our pledge of undying friendship. It'll make you feel better."

"I better go." Mercedes didn't exactly sound cheered up.

"I'll call Da."

"That'd be so great. You can tell her she should move. You can tell her it worked out great for you."

"Umm . . . I could."

"Mo, you're my best friend. No matter what."

They said good-bye, but when Mo tried to set the phone down, her fingers refused to uncurl. *No matter what.* Mo leaned against the chair. Every morning when her father got up and staggered toward the bathroom, he stubbed his toes on it. His *ye-ow* was her alarm clock these days.

Her hand was glued to the phone. Da. Mo's posture automatically improved, just thinking of her. She knew the number by heart.

"Hello?" said a thin voice.

"Da, it's me. Mo Wren."

"Give me strength!" Her voice plumped right up. Unlike Mercedes, it was easy to imagine Da: sitting in the corner of her couch, her reading lamp switched on, the crossword puzzle on her lap. "Child, I look across the street and think of you every day."

Mo sidled past the chair and into Dottie's room.

"That Sarah's so handy. Remember how your side door used to bang? And your front door used to stick? She took them both off and replaced them. Your house has two brand-new doors."

Feeling a little weak in the knees, Mo sat on the floor among Dottie's unpacked boxes.

"So," she said. "I guess they like Fox Street."

"Mrs. Petrone just gave that baby her first haircut. And Gertrude Steinbott!" Da chuckled. "She's knit Min an entire wardrobe by now. I doubt there's an ounce of pink yarn left in this entire city."

It was really cold on the floor.

"Let's see what else. Ms. Hugg got engaged! I hear she might be moving to Pittsburgh. Leo Baggott broke his collarbone playing Helen Keller. No sooner do I have two snowflakes on my front walk than Pi's out there shoveling. And he won't take a cent. That boy's a frog just waiting to be kissed."

"Erk!"

"Child? Did you say something?"

"What else, Da? Tell me more about the street."

"The old Kowalski place is up for rent again, in case you'd like to move back." She clucked her tongue. "That was meant as a joke, but it wasn't very funny, was it?"

Da hadn't even mentioned the hospital or her dining-room ceiling. The last thing she'd ever want was people feeling sorry for her, but still. Was it possible Mercedes had exaggerated a little? After all, she was dying for her grandmother to move down to Cincinnati. Could she be making Da's situation sound worse than it really was?

"I know why you called," Da said, and Mo pictured her lifting her chin that way all the Walcotts did. "I've been waiting for your report, scout. Tell me what it's like out there in that brave new world."

"It's . . . well." Suddenly Mo had a vision of Da's house with a 4 SALE sign out front. The porch stood empty and the windows were dark. She could almost hear the wind whistling around the corner, battering the old lilac. "It's hard, Da. It's like . . . well, our dining floor is crooked. And sometimes it feels like everything here is. Like I can't keep my balance. Like I'm just learning how to walk or something!"

"I know that feeling. After I lost my toes, I was afraid to take a step on my own. It was mortifying."

"Yeah," said Mo. "I mean, yes."

"You need to give it more time. You haven't lived there very long."

"It feels like it."

"Time creeps when you're young," Da said.

And then she didn't say anything else for a while. Mo pulled her knees up under her chin, trying to get warm. Why'd she blurt all that out? She was supposed to reassure Da that moving was great! Merce would be so disappointed if she knew. At last Da spoke.

"Whom does fortune favor?"

"The brave, Da."

"You're such a good student, Mo Wren." But Da sighed, as if she wasn't exactly sure about that lesson anymore. "I'm a little tired now. I appreciate your calling me."

By the time they said good-bye, Mo was worn out too. She rested her head on the box marked TREJER. Dottie's supposedly precious bottle collection! Mo closed her eyes, and before she knew it, Pi and Mercedes were helping unwrap the bottles, only instead of here, they were at the old Kowalski house. One of the bottles was full of plum pits, and when Mo picked it up, it turned into a tiny, wailing baby wrapped in a yellow blanket.

"Mo," someone said. "Mo!"

Mo opened her eyes to find her sister's grubby face an inch from hers.

"Don't cry," Dottie said.

"I'm not."

Dottie patted her head, as if she'd forgotten who was the little sister, and who was the big.

Shelter

Mo washed the new mugs and glasses and set them in a row beneath the mirror over the bar. When the walls were finally spackled and sanded, she stood on a ladder and helped her father paint the room Moonglow. It looked beautiful. They spent most of one morning scrubbing the floor, which was covered with a layer of grime so thick, they were surprised to discover the linoleum was actually green.

"That Corky wouldn't recognize soap if it bit him in the you-know-what." Mr. Wren put his hand to the small of his back, a gesture that was getting familiar. "All those years as a mud rat for the water department,

I never worked this hard."

Every night, he toiled at perfecting his burgers and omelets. He performed meat loaf experiments, trying hard-boiled eggs in the middle, or spicy ketchup on top. Mo didn't like meat loaf, no matter what, but Mr. Wren was convinced it would be a top seller. The Dottie Delight was spaghetti and two giant meatballs. The Mojo—that would purely and simply be the best burger in town. At first they ate in a corner of the kitchen, at their old table, but more and more they ate side by side at the bar, their reflections chewing along in the speckled mirror.

Mr. Wren's lists, written on sticky notes, covered half the mirror. Mo loved lists—making them, crossing things off them. Sometimes she'd pull on a jacket she hadn't worn for a while and discover a crumpled list in the pocket. Even if she could no longer remember which library book it was she'd returned, she'd still get satisfaction from the neat checkmark next to it.

But Mr. Wren? Back on Fox Street, he'd never made so much as a grocery list. They were always out of peanut butter or toilet paper. Dottie was used to eating her cereal with apple juice poured over it.

Now he'd papered the mirror behind the bar with sticky-note reminders. There was one for reading up on electricity, since Mr. Wren had discovered wires patched together with Scotch tape. And one for pricing toilets, since the bathrooms had to become handicapped accessible. Mr. Wren's handwriting was worse than his singing voice, so Mo couldn't decipher most of them. When notes unstuck themselves and fluttered to the floor, she taped them back up. Lists were supposed to be orderly things, but his swarmed around like yellow jackets at an ice-cream social.

"Lizards eat crickets," Dottie said, spinning her stool. "Just FYI."

Lately, Dottie talked in letters. AKA and ASAP and TMI. Even her best friend was named K.C.

Mr. Wren gathered up their plates and started for the kitchen.

"Lydia wants me to come over her house after school," Dottie called after him. "Can I?"

"You just went over her house," Mo said.

"OMG! That was Lauren, not Lydia!"

Mr. Wren paused, giving Mo a puzzled look. "Motown! How come you're not going over anybody's house?"

"Because. There's too much to do here. I like being here." The words didn't come out with the oomph she intended.

He set the dirty dishes on the bar and pulled his wallet from his pocket. "Tomorrow," he said, "you and a friend get doughnuts and cocoa."

Getting that bank loan didn't seem to have fattened his wallet any. He fingered the bills a moment, then pressed them into her hand.

"It's okay, Daddy. I don't need . . ."

He put a finger to her lips. "Remember—blue skies."

But when school let out the next afternoon, Dottie went home with Lydia, and Mo, as usual, walked across the park alone. She walked quickly, past the empty wading pool and empty benches, as if she had someplace exciting to go. Mo had never been the popular type. She'd always been content to have a school friend or two to eat lunch with and be her partner on projects. At the end of the day, she'd been happy to come back to Fox Street, where feeling lonesome was out of the question. And then all summer long, day in and day out, she'd had Mercedes.

Mo kept walking, zigzagging now, dirty snow squeaking under her feet. Her boots were too small and pinched her toes. So many of the girls here looked and acted older than she did, it was as if kids grew up faster on this side of the river. But so far the only parts of Mo that were growing were her feet and her hair. On Fox Street, whenever she needed a trim, she strolled up the street to visit Mrs. Petrone, who cut hair in her kitchen, and always just right. But here on East 213th, her hair just kept on growing.

Today Megan, a girl in her class, had asked Mo why she didn't do something different with it. It was long enough for a ponytail, suggested Megan, or French braids. Megan's own yellow hair lay flat on her head, as if it had run a long race and was exhausted. Was she trying to be friendly? Or just bossy? Mo wasn't sure.

The afternoon was so cold, even the faithful pigeon feeders had deserted their park bench. At least Mo's hair was good for one thing: keeping her neck warm. Every single day since they'd moved had been arctic. By now it was March, and spring was supposed to be whispering, "Here I come." Instead, frost coated the inside of Mo's bedroom window every morning. She had to scrape it with her thumbnail to see the skinny sidewalk tree, where the sparrows sat puffed up and miserable. Why didn't they migrate? Were they too stubborn or too dumb?

Mo stopped on the edge of the park and looked back over the winding path her boots had traced in the snow. If she went home, her father would want to know why she wasn't having fun with one of the zillion friends he was positive she'd made. When she told him, he'd be so disappointed.

But if she stayed out here, she'd freeze solid. She hugged herself, not knowing what to do. Ahead of her loomed the bus shelter. ADAM + EVA 4EVER, it said, and DICK LOVES JANE. The thing was one big valentine.

Inside she sat down on the orange plastic bench. The corpse of a spider hung high in one corner. The floor was covered with candy wrappers and squashed cups, right beneath the $300 FINE FOR LITTERING sign. There was a smell of something sweet, maybe the perfume of someone who'd recently waited here. Mo pulled up the collar of her jacket and snuggled into a corner. "Shelter" was the perfect word for this place. Like some big version of an umbrella, it protected you from rain and sun.

Except even umbrellas got to go places. The shelter stayed put. Like a tree.

Mo felt warmer now she was out of the wind. She found herself taking pleasure in the company of her own brain, the way she used to do back home when she sat beneath her old thinking spot, the plum tree.

raping a bit of icy frost off the wall, she thought how
nny it was that when it came to cakes, both frosting
d icing meant the same thing. When a bundled-
 woman stopped in the middle of the sidewalk,
ked off her yellow scarf, and began shouting into
 cell phone, Mo thought how being hot under the
lar was a good description of anger.

ut when the woman began to cry and dab her
s with the ends of the yellow scarf, Mo's mind wan-
ed to her mother's baggy yellow sweater. It had to
ut there somewhere. In science, Mr. Grimm had
ht them that matter is never destroyed. Even if an
ect got burned up, or pulverized, it didn't go away.
just became something else.

Like most really interesting ideas, this one was
multaneously wonderful and disturbing. Mo
anted to think about it more deeply, except that,
ven inside the shelter, she was too cold. When the
ellow-scarf woman jammed her phone back into her
urse and walked away, Mo almost missed her. Now
he was all alone. She wondered how long she'd have
to stay here, and if her father would ask about the
friend she'd spent the afternoon with. She'd have to
fib. She had no choice. She couldn't have him worrying about her.

And then Mo thought, *Our life is so messed up! W[e]* *both trying to keep the other one from worrying about* *We're worrying about worrying.*

Was this part of Corky's curse? That the memb[ers] of your own family turned into strangers? And y[ou] were forced to sit in a bus shelter all alone, as y[our] feet and fingers and head slowly, painfully, turne[d] blocks of ice?

"Where you going? Crazy?"

So
fu
an
up
ya
he
col
B
eye
der
be
taug
obj
It

ers
ou
our
to

Wishes

It must be brain freeze—there was no other explanation. Mo was actually happy to see that goofball Shawn. He gripped the edge of the shelter with his knees and shinnied halfway up.

"I'm just trying to get warm," she said.

"The best place for that's the Soap Opera." He slid back down. His feet were much too big for the rest of him, like his watch. "Come on."

The wind nipped and tugged at them as they hurried along the streets. But the Laundromat threw its warm arms around them the second they stepped inside. Homer was sound asleep in his usual seat, using a fat oven mitt for a pillow. Gilda, wearing a black dress and red high heels, stood beside Number Three, gesturing and talking to herself.

"She's an actress," Shawn explained. "She's got a big audition coming up, and the sound of the washers helps her concentrate."

Mo used some of her father's money to buy them treats from the vending machine. They were just in time to nab a spot on the plush van seat. Shawn pulled a copy of *Ripley's Believe It or Not!* from his backpack and settled in. When ten minutes went by and he hadn't looked up, Mo said, "Mr. Grimm should see you now."

"Mr. Grimm should be in this book," he said. "Most Boring Teacher in the History of Education." He picked a bit of candy out of his braces and went back to reading.

All this time Carmella was busy helping people, but at last she pulled up a kitchen chair. It was funny how small she was—Mo somehow remembered her being much taller. Her forehead gleamed with sweat.

"Number Six ate a lace tablecloth, and a car mechanic got Number Three all clogged up with grease. Thank goodness Homer was here to help. Number Eight went on overload again. The smoke detector went off, and Rosalie's baby started bawling and wouldn't stop." She patted her brow. Carmella even made sweating look beautiful. "How was school?"

Shawn didn't look up from his book. But Mo said, "Easy, compared to all that."

"Well, I didn't name it the Soap Opera for nothing. It's the human drama on a tiny stage, and I've been the director for years now. Hey, where's Red today?"

Mo bit the inside of her cheeks. Back on Fox Street, Dottie would stick to her like a little suckerfish. Mo couldn't get rid of her. Her sister was another thing she'd never counted on missing.

"She's busy."

Carmella tipped her chair back on two legs, a thing that always made Mo nervous.

"I spent a lot of my life wishing for a sister," she said. "Wishing on stars and wishbones and you name it."

From the sound of her voice, she was still wishing, though that didn't make any sense. Slowly she lowered her chair back to the floor and gave her head a quick shake, as if to clear her vision.

"Anyway," she said. "How's that daddy of yours managing? What's doing at Corky's?"

When Mo hesitated, Carmella pursed her lips.

"Sorry, sugar," Carmella said. "I should quit calling

it Corky's." A dryer was buzzing, and an argument over who got it next broke out, but Carmella ignored it. "What's it called now?"

"The Wren House."

"Oh, I like that."

"My father's working harder than he ever did his whole life."

"You'll see. Only good can come of that." A small gleam, like the candles people put in their windows at Christmastime, lit her eyes. She stood up. "Let's see if there's something here for you, little wren."

Watching her dig down in the bin in the corner, Mo nudged Shawn. "What is that, anyway?"

"The lost and found."

"You mean she gives away other people's stuff?"

"Only the stuff from deep down." Shawn closed his book and stretched his arms. "Stuff that's been there a long time."

Carmella surfaced holding a pale blue sweatshirt. Near the left shoulder, someone had embroidered a small black bird. When Carmella held it under Mo's chin, she got a whiff of pepper and vanilla, someone else's smell.

"Perfect!" said Carmella. "I'll wash it and have it ready next time you come."

A sweatshirt was just what Mo needed, since she still couldn't find her old favorite, the faded red one. And since the Wren House was always arctic. But how could she take something another person had lost?

Shawn stepped outside, but Carmella put a hand on Mo's arm.

"Sugar, you're just the friend Shawn needs," she said, her voice low and confiding. "He spends way too much time hanging out here with me."

Outside, the sidewalk was crowded with people eager to get home. Lights were coming on in the upstairs windows. Mo was better at finding her way around, but there were still so many doors and so many windows, belonging to people she'd never know. In one she saw a man standing by a stove, and in another a woman and a child watching TV together.

That outside-looking-in feeling socked her in the belly. The Soap Opera was its own little biosphere. After its summerlike air, winter's bite felt meaner than ever.

"I can't take that sweatshirt," she said, digging her hands into her pockets.

"Whaa?" Shawn tossed his hat into the air and caught it. "Carmella's right—it'll look fly on you."

Mo felt a little rush of pleasure. Shawn's habit of

saying the first thing that came into his head wasn't all bad.

"But what if someone comes back looking for it?" she said. "Or what if I wear it, and someone runs up to me and says, 'Hey, that's mine! I've been looking for it forever!'"

They were passing a building with scaffolding out front, and Shawn did a couple of pull-ups. The Soap Opera put him under a calm-down-and-concentrate spell, but the minute he left, *poof!*

"Carmella doesn't believe in stuff being lost," he said. "She says it all just goes around." He spun his hands around each other so fast they blurred. "Like life's one big revolving door. Or a boomerang. Not just stuff stuff, but the stuff we do. Put some kindness out there, and someday it'll come back to you. Be evil? Look out."

He backed up a few steps and took a running slide across a patch of ice, skidding into a teenager coming out of the used-book store. The boy made a grab for Shawn, but he ducked and sprinted away.

When Mo got home, Al was just locking his shop door.

"Hello," Mo said. "How are you?"

He jumped as if she'd said, "Stick 'em up."

"Sorry. I didn't mean to—"

"I'm not used to having neighbors." Thrusting his keys into his pocket, he gave a quick nod and scurried away.

What would Carmella say about Al? If he ever returned a kindness, it'd be front-page news.

Handsome

Went to pick up the Polka Dot, said the note stuck to the door.

Mo ratcheted up the thermostat, then sat in a booth and tried to do her homework. The furnace clanked, pretending to be hard at work, but the room didn't get any warmer. Where were those two, anyway? It was getting late. Laying down her pen, Mo went into the kitchen and found some leftover vegetable soup in the cavelike fridge. Back on Fox Street, she often heated up soup or made macaroni and cheese from the box. This industrial-sized stove, though, was strictly off-limits.

But Mo was hungry and chilly, and her family would be too, if they ever got home. Pulling the pot from the fridge, Mo set it on the stove. She rubbed her cold hands together. If her father came home and found supper waiting, he might see she was still his partner, someone he could trust. The stove had a row of big, greasy black knobs. Mo picked one and twisted it. Flames shot up from the wrong burner. But when she tried to turn the knob back, it wouldn't budge. The burner blazed like a giant iron spider that had caught on fire.

And then, to make things worse, the overhead lights slowly dimmed. The room grew darker, the stove brighter. Panicking, Mo tried the knob again, but the flames only leaped higher. As if Mo's own brain had lost power, she tried another knob, making two burning spiders, and then, who knows why, as if it would help, she lifted the heavy soup pot off the stove. At that same moment she heard footsteps, and the pot—the pot was her enemy too. It jumped from her hands and crashed to the floor.

Mr. Wren darted into the kitchen. In the dim light he didn't see the slippery spilled soup. "What the—?" Arms flailing, he fought off an invisible attacker. "Who the—?" He lurched to the stove and twisted the knobs. The flames vanished. The lights came back up, shining a spotlight on the mess.

"Uh-oh," said Dottie. Her arms were wrapped tight around a box with holes punched in its side.

Heart hammering, Mo picked up a mop. But Mr. Wren grabbed it from her.

"I can't believe it! What'd I tell you about that stove?"

Mo reached for the mop. "I'll clean it up."

"What were you thinking?" He held the mop out of her reach.

"I didn't know where you were so long! And it was cold in here, and I was getting hungry, and . . ."

"Here's where we were!" Dottie held out the box. "Guess what, Mo! Daddy let me . . ."

A look from Mr. Wren cut her off. Dottie bit her lip and hugged the box.

"This stove isn't for amateurs. As you found out the hard way." He shoved the mop through the splattered mess of tomatoes and carrots, then stopped and gave her a terrible look. "You could've done some real damage."

"So why don't we buy a better stove? Why do we have to use Corky's old piece of junk?"

"You have any idea what a restaurant-quality stove runs?"

"So what? We sold our house! Why don't we have more . . ."

"Quit changing the subject. You disobeyed. Big-time. That's not like you."

"Yeah, well, you're not like you, either! So we're even."

Curse. The word swooped like a bat across Mo's brain.

Mr. Wren thumped the mop upright. "Go on. Go help your sister."

Angry tears pushed at the back of Mo's eyes as she followed Dottie into the dining room. On the table where she'd been doing her homework sat a glass tank. Next to it was a big plastic sack that said PET UNIVERSE.

"Any minute now," Dottie whispered to the box as she set it down. From the bag she pulled out a fake rock with an electrical cord and a fake miniature palm tree. Once they'd gotten the rock plugged in, she told Mo, "You take the tank lid off." She began to undo the flaps on the box.

"Dottie, what's in . . ."

"Waaaa!"

Something small and hideous shot across the table. Without thinking, Mo grabbed it. A tiny, crazy pulse beat in her hand.

"Quick! The lid!"

Dottie whipped it off, and Mo lowered the creature into the tank. They swooped the lid back on.

Inside the tank, a scrawny lizard clung to the fake rock. Its bumpy skin was a sickly shade of gold. It was covered with dark spots, as if it wore a tiny leopard costume. After moving so fast, it suddenly grew so still, you could hardly tell it was alive.

Dottie pressed her nose to the glass.

"Here you are," she told it. "This is your new home."

It stared back, then shot out a snakelike tongue.

"How . . . why'd you pick him?" Mo imagined Pet Universe, all those kittens and hamsters and other fuzzy, cute, alive-acting things.

"He was on discount. We're not made of money, you know." Dottie put a finger to the glass and gave a lovesick sigh. "Isn't he so handsome?" She sat up in delight. "That's what I'll name him. Handsome Wren!"

The hot rock had to be plugged in at all times, since cold could kill geckos. Handsome ate worms and live crickets, and Dottie planned to teach him all kinds of tricks. Finding her crayons, she began to draw a picture to decorate his tank.

Mr. Wren came in carrying three cheeseburgers.

"I almost forgot, Mo!" Dottie said. "Guess what else? He already knows one really good trick. If a creditor tries to catches him, he just drops his tail off."

"*Pred*ator," Mr. Wren corrected. "Though come to think of it, what's the difference?"

Dottie, fountain of happiness, bubbled over. Nobody else could talk, supposing they wanted to. This was the best cheeseburger she ever tasted, and burgers and fries went together so well they ought to get married. To demonstrate, she made a fry and her burger kiss, *mm-wah*. And wait till she told K.C. about her pet. K.C. only had a dog that farted and drooled on you, and when she wrote about Handsome in her journal tomorrow, Ms. Thomas would say again what a wonderful addition Dottie was to their classroom family, and . . .

Meanwhile, Handsome Wren crouched on his rock, looking fragile as the old men on the park bench. What was he thinking? Just a few hours ago he'd lived one place, and now he found himself in a strange tank, not recognizing a single soul. Did he miss the old place? The other lizards he'd left behind? Was he trying to get back when he made his escape attempt? It was impossible to tell if a lizard was happy or sad. Not that it really mattered. He had no choice. Kids and pets had to go wherever they got taken.

"Mo," said Mr. Wren as she got up to clear the dishes. "Don't you have something to say?"

Mo lowered her eyes. "I'm sorry," she said.

"All right then."

I didn't say what for.

"You scared the stuffing out of me."

I wish we'd never moved here.

"I know you want to help, but that wasn't how."

I wish I had my old family back.

Turning away from her, he ruffled Dottie's hair. "Time for you to get ready for bed, little speck."

But first Dottie had to tape her drawing of beautiful tropical scenery to the side of Handsome's tank for his viewing pleasure. Too late, Mo realized her little sister had scribbled all over the back of her math worksheet.

Comfortable

Every morning before they left for school, Dottie made sure Handsome had fresh water and a breakfast cricket. This was a two-man operation, since Handsome could go from zero to a hundred miles an hour in the blink of his almond-shaped eyes. Mo hated being an accomplice to cricket murder. But if Handsome missed even one meal, his bumpy skin shrank against his toothpick bones. He was a sorry excuse for a pet, that was for sure.

"Make sure his rock is turned on," Mo said. "It's going to be cold today."

"Duh," said Dottie.

Instead of easing up, the winter dug in. Some mornings when her feet hit her icy bedroom floor, Mo longed for her own personal hot rock. In math, Mr. Grimm made them chart the month's temperatures and find the mean.

"Mean doesn't cover it," Shawn said to Mo in his usual much-too-loud whisper. "It's cruel and unusual punishment. This winter is unconstitutional."

Across the table, Megan giggled, then clapped her hand across her smile. When she leaned over, Mo could smell her sweet-sweet cherry Lip Smacker.

"I *mean*, how can you stand him?" she whispered.

"You seem to be increasingly popular, Mo," said Mr. Grimm. His voice said stern, but his eyes said gentle. "Which doesn't surprise me in the least." A couple of other girls turned to smile at Mo, who slid down in her seat.

At lunchtime, some of the girls stayed in to help Mr. Grimm put together the new math packets. Megan told Mo she should stay, too, and before Mo knew it, she was sitting at a table sorting paper and whacking a stapler. The other girls were big talkers. Their conversation skipped like a rock across a sun-spangled pond. Indoor soccer; what kind of cell phone they'd get when they were finally allowed; whether a koala, hedgehog, or baby seal was the world's cutest animal.

Mo had cataloged Megan with the more popular girls, so she was surprised by how bashful she turned out to be. She kept pushing her tired-out yellow hair behind her ear and picking at her chapped lips. How had they gotten chapped, with all that Lip Smacker? When her stapler jammed up, Megan gave a nervous giggle.

"I'm so dumb!" she said.

"Don't say that," a tall girl named Mary told her. "Low self-esteem is not attractive."

Mo took the stapler and fixed it. Megan gave her a grateful smile.

"Your little sister's my cousin's friend," Mary told Mo. "K.C."

"K.C.'s her idol," said Mo. "She wants us to call her D.W. now, instead of Dottie."

That made everybody laugh, and Mo, encouraged, went on, "We used to call her Wild Child, but she won't let us since she's so grown-up and cool." She turned to Megan. "You have any sisters?"

"No," said Megan. "But my little brother thinks he's a knight. He has this sword he won't take off, even in the bathtub."

"Aargh!" Asha jangled her bracelets. "My brother's

a T. rex! He keeps begging our mother to feed him raw meat."

"Well, my other brother's sixteen, and his room stinks like a dinosaur lives there!" Megan's cheeks went pink with the excitement of suddenly being in the middle of things. "Boys are so repulsive!"

"They're aliens!"

"Primates!"

"Boys should get declared another species!"

"I beg your pardon," said Mr. Grimm from his desk.

When the bell rang, the rest of the class came in. Shawn was last, straggling along, blowing on his fingers. He must have lost another pair of gloves.

"Don't look now," Asha told Mo, "but here comes your sweetie."

Mary threw her arms in front of Mo in a warding-off way. "Quit pestering her!" she ordered Shawn. "She doesn't want to hang with you anymore!"

The air around Shawn ceased its whirring and buzzing. A split second later he spun around and knocked into a desk, setting pencils and papers cascading to the floor.

"Whoa!" he cried, wheeling his arms. "Avalanche! Look out!" He pretended to lose his footing and collapse on the floor.

"That was so funny I forgot to laugh," said one of the boys, stepping over him.

Shawn stayed on the floor till Mr. Grimm made him get up. The rest of the afternoon didn't get any better for him. He sharpened his pencil till it was barely an inch long, and he had to borrow from Mo. In music he blew his recorder so loud, no one would stand next to him. When the day finally ended, he was first out the door. And yet when Mo stepped outside, she nearly collided with him. He was waiting on the step, his bare hands tucked into his armpits, his hair wafting in the wind.

"You need to come to the Soap Opera," he said. "Carmella's been asking about you."

"Oh, right," said Mo. But Carmella's words whispered in Mo's ear. "You're just the friend Shawn needs. He spends way too much time hanging out here with me."

At the crosswalk, Mary, Asha, and some of the other girls who walked home stood waiting with Mary's mother. Mary was pointing across the park, doing a robot imitation.

"Doughnuts!" she said. "Must. Have. Doughnuts!"

The crossing guard tooted his whistle, and the cluster of bright jackets and cute hats jiggled across the street, then swerved in the direction of the Pit Stop. Mo imagined running and catching up. Imagined them making room for her as they bunched in front of the counter, agonizing over glazed or chocolate or jelly.

Shawn looked from Mo to the girls and back again. With a grunt, he bolted toward the crosswalk. The guard grabbed the back of his jacket.

"Slow down, young man!"

Now he was in for a lecture from the crossing guard, too. Shawn's head slumped forward. He didn't look up as he and Mo crossed the street side by side. But when they reached the other side, she stepped in front of him.

"You go to Carmella's every single day?"

"Umm. Affirmative."

"How come you don't do any other stuff? Like join the science club, the way Mr. Grimm keeps begging you?"

"Mr. Grimm!" Shawn staggered backward. "He only wants me to come so he can torture me further. Mr. Grimm hates my guts!"

"Well, what about basketball? You shoot a million invisible baskets every day. Why don't . . ."

Shawn reached for his hat, then remembered he wasn't wearing one. Grabbing a chunk of gritty frozen snow, he threw that into the air instead.

"I like it at Carmella's." He caught the snow and tossed it again, higher this time. "It's comfortable. Nobody bothers me." Higher yet. "I don't have to worry what people . . ."

This time he missed. The ice ball hit the ground and smashed. Shawn rubbed his hands together.

"What people think or say. It's like I'm wrapped in super armor or something. Safe from everything. I wish I could stay there all the time. "

How could Mo argue? Shawn was describing the very feeling she longed for herself. It was the feeling of being wrapped inside the yellow sweater.

"Carmella really did ask about you. Who knows why?" He balled his bare hands into fists and marched away. After a moment, Mo marched behind him, fitting her boot prints into his.

At the Laundromat, Homer waved them over. He was drinking from a mug that said I ♥ CHIHUAHUAS.

"You missed it," he told them. "A really tall woman just left."

"How tall?" Mo asked.

"When it rains, she gets wet an hour before everybody else."

"Homer," called Carmella. "Drink your tea—it's

97

full of antioxidants."

"I thought oxygen was good for you," he said, but obediently drained his cup.

"And don't forget," Carmella added, "you promised to change those lightbulbs for me."

Homer gave a two-fingered salute and went to get the ladder.

Moments later, Gilda rushed in, her earrings like wind chimes in a hurricane.

"I got the part! I'm Blanche!" She jumped up on a chair and clasped her hands to her chest. "I have always depended on the kindness of strangers," she declared in a luscious Southern drawl. And then, somehow, a real tear trickled down her cheek.

Mo applauded, along with everyone else. Shawn settled in with his *Ripley's* while she watched a TV cooking demonstration on mashed potato variations. The cheesy ones looked so good, and not that hard. Too bad she was still angry at her father. She might have copied down the recipe.

Back home she found Dottie sitting at the bar. In his tank beside her, Handsome seemed to be watching *X-Men* as attentively as she was.

"Where's Daddy?"

Without turning her head, Dottie said, "He went . . .

he went . . . I forget. Just for a minute, someplace."
A commercial came on, and she twirled her stool.
"Look, you got a letter."

Lying among the bills—Mr. Wren used the bar for
his desk—was an envelope addressed to her. "East
213th Street" was written in precise, uniform cur-
sive, the t's like the slashes of a miniature sword. Da's
teacher handwriting, for sure. But someone else had
written Mo's name, in print so tiny, the mail carrier
must have needed a magnifying glass.

The writing inside was just as minuscule. The words
huddled at the top of the paper, leaving a vast empty
space beneath.

Dear Mo,
How are u? Da says fine. Are u really?
I found that red shirt you like in your driveway. I'm keep-
ing it for u.
Urs truly,
Pi Baggott
P.S. I can do a 180 now.

"He should have put SWAK," Dottie said, looking
over her shoulder. "That means Sealed with a Kiss,
FYI."

"MYOB," Mo told her. Folding up the letter, she hurried through the door that said PRIVATE. Upstairs, she knocked her shin against the green armchair but hardly noticed. At last, sitting on her bed, she unfolded the letter and read it again.

I'm keeping it for u. Her heart did a little sparkler imitation. He missed her, she could tell. Not that she took any pleasure in imagining him gloomy and lonesome. At least, not much pleasure. Just a little. If his feet grew heavy when he passed her old house, or if his thoughts flew to her when he pulled off a perfect 180, well.

Kneeling beside her dresser, she opened the bottom drawer and moved aside a pair of pajamas. There they were, her Fox Street treasures. First she unwrapped the tissue paper that protected the woody little plum pit. Almond shaped and dark gold, it reminded her of Handsome's eyes. Next she picked up the knit bag and unknotted the drawstring. Lifting it to her face, she breathed in the perfume of long-lost summer.

And now Pi's letter. Just when she'd begun to feel that maybe, just maybe, she could belong in this new place, here was another reminder of Fox Street. Homesickness pierced her, a sliver too deep to ever tweeze out.

But the next reminder, when it came, was worst of all. She had a promise that her old favorite shirt was waiting for her back there. Maybe Pi had put it in a drawer of his dresser, for safekeeping.

Comfortable. That was Shawn's word for how he felt at Carmella's. But comfortable was too flimsy a word for Fox Street. Like saying the earth was round, or trees had leaves—it was only the beginning.

The Blue Sweatshirt

Powdered sugar drifted down on the park. A group of little kids with name tags pinned to their jackets lay on their backs making snow angels while their teacher clapped for them. Dottie scooped up a mittenful and ate it.

"Hello, Shawnster," she said as he jumped out from behind a tree.

Shawn walked backward in front of them. He still hadn't gotten a new hat, and his hair glittered with snow.

"By the way." Dottie stopped and put her hands

on her hips, one of her new, infuriating habits. "Mo already has a boyfriend. Back home. He writes her love letters."

Shawn looked stupefied. "So?"

"Just a tip to the hip, as Ms. Thomas says."

"It's my duty to inform you," Shawn said, "that according to the laws of big sisterhood, Mo is now required to beat you up." He turned to Mo. "I'm here to help, if you want."

Dottie fake screamed and started to run. Her first-grade backpack was so light, it flopped up and down on her back.

"There's only one safe place!" Speedy as he was, Shawn lapped circles around her. "The Soap Opera. Go!"

Today Carmella was all about scarves—tied in her hair, knotted at her throat, lassoing her hips.

"Red!" she cried. "What's up?"

"I got a gecko! I'm teaching him tricks. He already knows 'Lie down.'"

"He's a genius!"

"I read that book you gave me," Dottie said. "To make sure I'm doing everything right. My sister helps too." She patted Mo's arm. "She cleans out his poop.

It looks just like dried-up chocolate ice cream."

"My my my. Lizard poop. That's a true test of sisterhood. You two . . ." Carmella's gaze lingered on them; then she poked her lip and turned away.

The place grew busier and busier as afternoon spun into evening. A ballpoint pen left in a shirt pocket exploded during the spin cycle, and all the guy's clothes turned baby blue. When a teenage girl started screaming and stopped her washer to fish out her cell phone, Carmella clucked and said it must be Forgetful Friday. Round and round people's clothes twirled, bright cloth fish in their big aquariums.

"There's a guy with like five hundred tattoos," Shawn said, looking up from his book. "He has them between his toes. On his eyelids. That is one dedicated dude."

A good-looking man, half again as tall as Carmella, asked for advice on the dark, oily stain on his shirt. Pearls might have been dropping from her lips, the way he bent toward her, catching every word. Before long he was explaining the stain was tamari sauce. Did Carmella like Thai food? Carmella replied she liked any kind of food she didn't have to make, since cooking was the one thing on this earth Carmella couldn't do. What do you know—the man loved to cook! Especially for other people!

"He's probably going to be her boyfriend now," said Dottie.

"She's already got a bazillion." Shawn shut the *Ripley's* and yawned. "I got this book memorized."

"It's about time you read something else," Dottie told him. "Ms. Thomas says variety is the hot sauce of life."

Homer left for supper at the church on the next block. As Mo, Dottie, and Shawn got ready to go, Carmella brought a pair of lost and found earmuffs and settled them on Shawn's head. Then she handed Mo a plastic bag.

Inside was the blue sweatshirt, washed, fluffed, and folded. When Mo held it up, a fragrance heavy and light, sweet and sharp filled the air. It was honey and lemons, roses and just-cut grass, all mixed with something pure and clear as water tumbling over rocks.

"Umm," Mo said, sniffing.

"That's the smell of something once lost and now found," Carmella said with a wink.

Something both pretty and warm. Until Mo could claim her old red sweatshirt, it was just what her wardrobe needed. Still, she was reluctant to take it.

"It's your turn," Carmella said, reading Mo's mind. "You'll see."

Shoulder to shoulder, the three kids walked home. The days were getting longer now, the light stretching on both ends like pastel-colored taffy. Shawn told how Carmella's parents had both died when their car crashed in a freak blizzard. That made Dottie slide her hand into Mo's. So Carmella didn't have parents, and as they knew, no sister, either. She lived upstairs, and every morning she got dressed, brewed herself some tea, and came down to work. Most everybody knew her, some for years, some just for the few months they rented in the neighborhood.

Here Shawn paused to crouch and pet a gray cat sitting in a doorway. The cat flopped over, paws tucked up, and rolled from side to side. Its purr said it had never gotten a better belly rub in all its nine lives.

"I'm never living all by myself," said Dottie. "Not even when I'm grown up."

Shawn stood back up. The furry lost and found earmuffs stood out on his head like he was part teddy bear.

"Carmella's happy." He snapped off a dagger-sized icicle hanging from a stop sign. "She's like a wizard.

People walk into her place loaded down with smelly clothes and walk out all fresh and clean."

But was she as happy as Shawn said? Every time the talk turned to sisters, something came over her. Life had played Carmella a dirty trick, not giving her one. What a perfect sister she'd make!

"You know she'll be there, anytime you're looking for her," he said. "Like the moon."

"The moon travels," Dottie said. "Ms. Thomas says . . ."

"Okay. Like the sun." Bending backward, he javelined the icicle into the air. It crash-landed at the feet of a woman wearing a fur hat the size of a bucket.

"What in the world!" she yelped.

"I'm outta here!" Shawn took off.

No sooner had they turned onto East 213th than Dottie began to run, the way she always did. Their father must have been watching for them, because he stepped outside and raised his arm as if Dottie were a long fly ball he was preparing to catch. When Mo got closer, she saw he was holding the phone.

"For you," he said. But when Mo reached for it, he pressed the phone to his chest.

"Is something wrong?" Mo asked.

"Da's in the hospital." His hand cupped her

shoulder. "Mercey's really upset. Think you can handle it?"

"Yes."

"That's what I thought." He pushed open the door. Still wearing her jacket and backpack, Mo took the phone. Mr. Wren led Dottie into the kitchen.

"Hi, Merce!"

Her best friend started crying.

"Merce? What happened? Is she . . ."

"She slipped on the ice. She was on her way to Abdul's and she fell, and nobody was around." Her voice quavered. "How can that be? Somebody's always out on Fox Street!"

Mo pictured Da lying alone on a sidewalk, in pain. Calling out, and nobody coming. In some terrible way, this felt like something she'd already seen, like a bad dream come true.

"Is she . . . ?"

"She doesn't know how long she lay there. Finally that woman who moved into your house came along. Sarah? She called 911." Mercedes gave another sob. "If only Da had moved in with us! This never would have happened!"

Mo's mind flew to the last time she'd talked to Da,

when Da had asked her what the brave new world was like.

"She broke her arm. She had to have surgery and get pins in it. And they're still not sure—she might— she was out in the cold so long—she could lose some more toes."

Mo sank into a booth. She pulled off her backpack and clutched it like a shield. The last time they'd talked, Mo had told Da how hard moving away was. Instead of reassuring Da, and urging her to move in with Mercedes, she'd poured out all her own troubles.

"I . . . I'm so sorry!" she said.

"Monette's with her now. I begged to go too, but she said no. She left me stuck here with Three-C."

Mo squeezed her backpack tight. A bit of blue popped through the half-open zipper. Carmella's sweatshirt. Pulling it out, Mo burrowed her nose into its lost and found perfume.

"That family?" Mercedes sniffled. "Sarah and Min and whatever the husband's named? They called to tell us what happened. They're really nice. Oh, Mo." Mecedes drew a long, shuddery breath. "I feel better just talking to you."

Mo swallowed. Her best friend wouldn't say that if

109

she knew it was Mo's fault Da had gotten hurt.

"Say something," Mercedes begged.

"Could you . . . could you give Da a message for me?"

"Oh, Mo." Mercedes' voice quavered. "You know I will."

"Tell her I said to remember, fortune favors the brave."

"She'll like that."

Mercedes promised to call Mo again soon.

Mo hung up but stayed slumped in the booth. The picture of Da lying hurt on an icy sidewalk wouldn't go away, and she realized she was shivering. She tugged the blue sweatshirt over her head. Its scent wrapped her in its arms, soothing her.

That night, Mo couldn't sleep. Her painted-shut window rattled in the wind. She thought of Homer sleeping in the shelter, Carmella all alone above the Laundromat, Da in a hospital room. From outside came the muffled sound of a dog barking, over and over. Was he lost? On a night like this? Why didn't anyone come find him?

Mo pushed back her covers and tiptoed across the cold floor, around the green armchair, and down the steps. Flicking on the light, she checked that

Handsome was all right. His silly starfish feet, his funny little leopard suit! The two of them stared at each other, unblinking. Was it really true, as Dottie's book claimed, that lizards didn't get lonesome? When she put her face close to the glass, he shot out his pink tongue.

"Handsome? Lonesome?" she asked.

Handsome slowly raised his foot, as if trying to tell her something. But what?

Back upstairs, Mo took the blue sweatshirt back out of the drawer and pulled it on over her pajamas. As she wiggled her arms into the sleeves, the dog stopped barking at last. Slipping under the covers, she discovered Dottie had crawled into her bed. Her little sister snuggled up against her, and Mo drifted into sleep.

The Curse, Part Two

"You're wearing that sweatshirt again," said Megan. "Not to criticize or anything, but it's the third time this week."

"It's comfortable. I like it."

Spring break would begin that Friday. Mo was counting the hours so desperately, you'd think she had something to look forward to. Outside, the crusty old snow still hid the grass. At home, her father continued to go through boxes of Band-Aids as fast as Mo could replace them.

Just last night, the electricity had dimmed, then surged, then gone out completely. Down in their dungeon basement, Mr. Wren had fiddled with the circuit breakers, calling up the stairs to Mo, "Now? How about now?" At last he'd coaxed the lights back on, but the freezer still refused to cooperate. They'd had to set their meat outside the back door in a cooler. Way past midnight, Mo woke to hear him trudging upstairs. She cringed, knowing he'd forget and stub his toe on the green chair, and sure enough, *"Yeow!"* Why couldn't he ever remember? This morning he had dark circles under his eyes, and his coffee breath smelled as strong as if he'd chewed raw beans.

Maybe, Mo thought, *maybe that's the curse.* Stubbornness. If there was ever a place that resisted getting reinvented, it was Corky's. But her father was just as pigheaded. She'd never in her life seen him work so hard at something. To tell the truth, back on Fox Street, she'd wondered if he *could* work hard. Now he'd proved he was capable, but what if he was working at the wrong thing? The impossible thing?

The clamor of the lunchroom rose up around her. When she was home, she felt angry at her father, but away from him, she missed him. Did that make sense?

Mo nuzzled her chin down inside her sweatshirt. Its scent was fading, but if she sniffed hard, she could still catch it.

"Are you getting a cold?" Megan asked.

"Umm, I don't think so."

"Maybe we could go shopping together over spring break," Megan said. "My mom could take us to Crocker Place."

Mo was so startled, she nearly lost her grip on her tray. This was the first official Eastside Park School invitation she'd gotten. She recognized it for a big moment, even as she wished Megan had said, "Maybe we can watch a movie." Or "Maybe we can bake cookies." Mo was as pitiful at shopping as her father was at home repair. Plus, where would she ever get the money?

"Okay," she said.

"Sweet!" Megan beamed. "This Saturday. And you can come over my house afterward. I'll teach you to French braid."

Mary, Asha, and the other girls smooshed together, making room for them. At the next table, Shawn wriggled around as if his skin was an especially bad fit today. After Mo threw away her garbage, she stopped beside him.

"What time is it in Tokyo?"

"Eleven-thirty p.m.," he said, not even consulting his watch. "And five-thirty p.m. in Niger. I have my tutor today, so I have to skip Carmella's. Please don't weep."

And Dottie had Daisy Scouts. Mo would be on her own.

At three o'clock Cleveland time, Shawn cometed through the door. Filing behind, Mo listened to Mary and Asha talk about Pet Universe, where they had kittens you were allowed to hold.

"You like kittens?" Asha asked Mo as they crossed the street.

"Well, duh," said Mary, laughing. "You might as well ask her if she's a normal human being!"

Were they inviting her to come along? Should she run home and tell her father? But what if they weren't really, or what if she tagged along and when it was only the three of them, Mo's tongue tied itself in a knot? Should she take the risk? She had to decide right this minute.

As if the answer might appear among the graffiti, Mo looked across the grass at the bus shelter. Someone with big feet and no hat was shinnying up its edge.

"There he is," said Mary, following Mo's eyes. "Your faithful shadow!"

"He's actually kind of cute *looking*," said Asha. "If only he didn't have the most annoying personality ever."

"Well." Mo remembered the day she'd been sitting in the shelter, half frozen, and he'd come along to take her to the Soap Opera. As much as she longed to go see the kittens, Mo felt a little bridge arcing across the frozen park, linking her and him. "He's not so bad. I mean, if you saw him outside school, you'd . . ."

"School's more than enough for me!" said Mary. "You're too nice, Mo."

"Yeah," said Asha. "There's such a thing, you know."

They walked away, kicking up sparkly sprays of snow with their boots. Mo stomped in the opposite direction. As she approached, Shawn's eyebrows lifted into igloo shapes.

"Yo," he said, fake surprised. "It's you."

"You said you had your tutor today."

"I got time to check in at the S.O. first." He kicked a squashed coffee cup. "Carmella worries if I don't." He waited a beat. "You're coming, right?"

For once Shawn didn't speed ahead but tried to match his pace to hers. They took a right, a left, another right. They were almost there when Shawn stopped and pointed.

"Hey, it's open!"

It was a little place next to the hardware. The

COMING SOON sign they'd passed for weeks had been replaced by NOW OPEN—THE ROBIN'S EGG CAFE. Peering in, they saw a cozy room with pretty blue walls. People crowded the tables or bent to choose from a glass case brimming with sandwiches, muffins, and other delicious-looking things. When a woman opened the door and stepped outside, the smell of butter and cinnamon made a beeline straight for their noses.

"They're giving away free samples," she said, pulling on her gloves. "And everything's perfectly scrumptious!"

Shawn dove for the door, but Mo caught his arm.

"We can't go in there," she said. "It's the enemy. It's direct competition for the Wren House."

"One nanobite? How much can it hurt? I mean, considering the you-know-what?"

"You're always talking about the curse!" she cried. "What do you really know about it, anyway? Did you just make it up or is it real? I need to know."

Shawn shot an invisible basket, pulled his pockets inside out, stooped to pick up the junk that fell out. At last he gave up and looked Mo in the eye.

"It's what people say. I'm not sure if that makes it real or not."

"What else happened there? Besides Corky vanishing in the night?"

"Before him, it was an Italian restaurant called Bruno's. Bruno hated kids. He was nice if you were with your parents. Otherwise he'd tell you get lost or he'd grind you in his sausage maker. One night everybody who ate there got sick, and people started saying he used bad meat, and after a while he went out of business."

"How about before Bruno?"

"That was this sweet old lady named Granny Bumps. Or so she said. She ran a pie shop. One night a robber broke in, and she whomped him in the head with a hot blueberry pie. Only when the cops came, they took her in too. Her real name was Lola, and she was wanted for running a gambling ring."

Shawn slumped against the wall. Sticking to one topic this long was wearing him out. Still, he forged on.

"Before that, it was a whole long line of people. It stretches back before I lived here. Maybe before I was born." The corners of his mouth twitched. "Oh, yeah. There was another guy, I think his name was Bob. Bob was so stingy, he refused to even pay anyone a compliment. He . . ."

Mo clapped her hands over her ears. "That's enough," she said. "More than enough!"

The Robin's Egg door swung open again, releasing a river of sugar and spice. In spite of herself, Mo's mouth watered. Could the curse of Corky's be that it attracted the wrong people, over and over? If only she knew what had happened to Corky. Why had he fled in the middle of the night? And where had he gone? A bus rumbled by, headed toward the river and the other side of town. If the Wrens had to leave, there was only one place on earth she could imagine them going.

Shawn consulted his watch. "I'm dead. Tell Carmella I'm at my tutor's!" As he raced away, he yelled over his shoulder, "We'll bust that curse! We can burn stuff and bury stuff and my stepsister has these crystals and . . ."

Mo's thoughts rattled around her head like stones inside a can. She should go home, but somehow, next thing she knew, she was pushing open the door of the Soap Opera.

Number Three was pulled out from the wall. Gripping a wrench, Homer regarded its insides with the same pleasure Shawn did the photo of the man who could hold eleven diamondback rattlers in his mouth at once. Mo didn't see Carmella till her head poked up from behind the machine.

"Can you give us a hand here, sugar?" she called.

"Probably a clogged drain line," Homer said, passing the wrench to Mo. "Like to learn some plumbing? It's a useful skill." He ambled across the room.

On the floor, a big metal toolbox gaped wide, displaying pliers and hammers and screwdrivers of every size. Carmella was investigating a black rubber hose sticking out from the bottom of the washer.

"Something probably got caught between the tubs," she said. "Poor old Number Three just spins its wheels but can't pump." She laughed. "Reminds me of some people I know. Get a grip on this hose, sugar. That's right." She selected a pair of needle-nose pliers from her toolbox.

"I didn't know you fixed the machines too," Mo said.

"Homer taught me. He's a jack-of-all-trades." She nodded across the room, where he pulled a tattered tablecloth from the lost and found and settled it capelike around his shoulders. "Just pray it's not the pump. That I can't fix, and I don't really want to buy a new one." Carmella poked the pliers around inside the hose. Ironing her lips into a straight line, she regarded the ceiling. "I could've been a surgeon, if I could stomach the sight of blood," she said.

"How'd you ever learn how to do so much stuff?"

"Trial and error. A professional's just an amateur who didn't quit. Aha!"

Mo watched Carmella draw out the pliers. Dangling from the tip was a black bra.

"The culprit!" She flung it into a trash can.

"Not the lost and found?" Mo asked.

"Now and then, a thing comes to the end of the line!"

Mo watched Carmella rehook the hose, check and clean some other parts, squirt oil here and there, and at last screw on the back panel. It was true—she'd make a thorough, gentle doctor. Once her patient was all patched up, she and Mo pushed it back into place.

"By the way," said Carmella with a wiggle of her eyebrows, "that sweatshirt looks adorable on you." She switched the machine on for a test run. "Shawn went to his tutor, I hope?"

How could Carmella keep so many things straight? It was as if she stored knowledge not just inside her head, but in special compartments in her fingers and toes too. When Number Three commenced to both spin and pump, she unlocked the vending machine and selected two bags of chips. They sat side by side on the van bench, feet tucked under them.

"This is the definition of cozy." Carmella ate her chips one by one, licking her fingers after each. "And where's Big Red?"

"Daisy Scouts."

"The way she looks up to you!" Carmella considered the fringe on the bright scarf twisted in her long hair. "Like you not only hung the moon but every single star, one by one. No, like you're the moon itself!"

"You might need glasses, Carmella."

"Ha. Joke all you like, little wren. Just as long as you know how lucky you are!" Carmella's feet hit the floor with a thump. "All right. Time for me to get back to work."

"Carmella," Mo blurted, "do you believe in being under a curse?"

Carmella sat back. She carefully selected another chip and considered it. Mo began to feel better, knowing Carmella was preparing a lecture on such a ridiculous, ignorant notion.

"I do," Carmella said. "I surely do."

Mo's mouth went so dry, she couldn't swallow. Bits of chip lay on her tongue like dust.

"Carmella's under one herself."

"You?" Mo managed the one word.

Carmella nodded. She creased and folded her empty chip bag as if it were a piece of laundry. "It's a bad one. I don't think I'll ever break it." Her beautiful, gold-flecked eyes dimmed.

The door kept opening and closing. The after-work rush was under way, and Carmella stood up.

"Don't ask what just came over me. Carmella never talks this way." She gave Mo a sad smile. "Thanks for listening, sugar. But just forget what I said, okay?"

And she swept away to help her many customers.

Don't Worry

On Friday, the last afternoon before spring break, Mr. Grimm showed the class a movie. Everyone had already seen it, plus it was for kids far younger, but Mo considered this a symbolic gesture. Even teachers recognized a day for rejoicing.

"I'll call you tomorrow," Megan said before she hurried to meet her babysitter. "I can't wait!"

"Me either," said Mo, though she'd still rather do most anything than try on clothes. And she still had no idea where she'd get the money to buy them.

Some kindly giant hand had found the sun's plug and connected it. If you closed your eyes and tilted your face, the backs of your eyelids prickled with color, and warmth brushed your brow and cheeks. In the park, green grass islands dotted the snowy sea.

Dottie picked up a fallen, shiny-wet branch.

"I wish we were going someplace," she said, dragging it behind her. "K.C.'s family goes to this really cool indoor water park."

"I guess you wish you had another family," Mo teased.

"No." Dottie broke the stick in half and scratched her head with it. "Just sometimes."

Mo couldn't believe it. Once upon a time, Dottie's biggest fear was whether Mo would always be her sister. But that was ancient history, apparently. Dottie tossed the stick over her shoulder and started walking in the wrong direction.

"Where do you think you're going?"

"The Robin's Egg is giving away free samples all week. They got these sugar cookies that are to die for." At the mention of sugar, Dottie's face softened. "You should come too, Mo."

"That's the enemy! We can't go there."

"The lady's really nice. She wears purple nail polish."

"We can't give her our business, and that's that. Besides, this isn't Fox Street. You're not allowed to go places alone."

The two old friends were back on their bench for the first time in weeks. Both wore binoculars around their wrinkly necks. Pigeons clustered at their feet, making greedy, chortling sounds. In the snow their tracks looked like a line of miniature jet planes, swooping and curving.

Dottie pulled a bubble-gum-flavored ChapStick out of her pocket. Where'd she gotten that? ChapStick was on the forbidden list, since she could never resist eating it. Now she smeared it over her lips and gave them a satisfied lick.

"That was ye olden days," she said. "I'm not a little kid anymore."

"Make me laugh!"

"FYI, I know my way around this neighborhood way better than you do."

"Do not!"

"Do so!"

"Do not!"

"Do so!"

The men's heads swiveled back and forth on their turkey necks.

"Fine!" yelled Mo. Her good mood went up in steam. "I've had it with you! Go ahead! See if I care! Go to the moon!"

"I wish!"

Dottie marched away. The men leaned forward, regarding Mo with expectant faces. Surely she wouldn't let such a young, not to mention demented, girl wander off on her own? Embarrassed, Mo turned away, but instead of following her sister, she made straight for the bus shelter.

The floor was littered with cigarette butts, as if there'd been a party, or as if one person had sat waiting way too long. The sun heated the place up, and Mo unzipped her jacket. Scrunched into the corner, she tried counting to a hundred. She was up to eighty-seven when a bus pulled up, brakes hissing. The sign said 18 PARADISE. Pushing open the door, the driver looked down at Mo. It took her a moment to realize what he was waiting for.

"Oh, no," she cried. "I'm not going anywhere! I'm just taking shelter here."

"Poor baby," he said, and pulled the door shut.

Embarrassed all over again, Mo stood up. Even the shelter wasn't a shelter today. One of the pigeon men lowered his binoculars and waggled his finger at her as she trudged by.

Dottie was not at the Robin's Egg. Not the Soap Opera, either.

"She hasn't been in," said Carmella, her brow creasing like a dusky fan. "Want Homer to help look?"

"It's okay," Mo said, aiming for a lighthearted tone. "It's not the first time I ever hunted for her."

But a little belt of worry drew itself around her heart. Back on Fox Street, she'd have known exactly where to look, but here? She didn't know the names of all Dottie's friends, much less where they lived. She peered down the street, with its jumble of people, doors, and signs. Dottie was barely tall enough to see over the parked cars, and she wasn't what you'd call an excellent reader. It'd be easy for her to lose her bearings.

Not to mention, after all those years of living on dead-end Fox Street, you couldn't trust her to look both ways when she crossed a street.

The worry belt tightened another notch. Mo knew she should go home and tell her father. He'd jump in the car and find her. But as clearly as if he stood before her, Mo saw how disappointed and upset he'd look when she told him what she'd done. What was wrong with her? What had happened to the dependable, trustworthy girl she'd been? What in the world had come over her?

A guilty-looking orange cat slunk by. Feeling queasy, Mo blundered up and down the long streets. Once or twice she lost her bearings herself, but one foot kept putting itself in front of the other, till she found herself back by the Robin's Egg. She'd traveled a circle, or a rectangle, or some shape with no name, and come right back where she'd started. Sisterless.

Think. Mo swallowed hard. Think.

But all she could do was wonder. What should she do? Why were so many things her fault? How had life gotten so messed up and unfair?

Wondering was not thinking. It was only one letter removed from wandering.

The sun slid down the sky, taking all the day's hopeful warmth with it. A grouchy man shuffled toward her on the sidewalk. He wore large rubber boots with buckles. Fountains of hair spurted from his ears. Al! Al the shoe guy! Mo was overcome with gratitude to recognize someone, even him.

"Al! It's me! Your neighbor!"

In reply, Al tucked his whiskery chin against his shoulder. A harrumphing sound escaped him, and he pointed over his shoulder.

Close on his rubber heels came Dottie, her head down and her thumb in her mouth. Clutched to her chest was a bag that said PET UNIVERSE.

"There you are!" Mo grabbed her.

Whomp. Dottie's head drove into Mo's stomach.

"Are you okay?" Mo asked. Dottie's head went up and down. "That's too bad," Mo told her, "because I have to kill you."

"I remembered Handsome's out of crickets." Dottie sniffled. "I was only trying to be a good pet owner. The guy at Pet Universe is so nice—he said I could pay next time. But when I came out, I got backwarded. I think they moved the door, or something."

Dottie's scarf dragged on the ground. Mo wrapped it around her sister's neck.

"Please don't strangle me!"

Mo's heart, half strangled itself, began to beat normally once more. Looking down at her sister, she thought of Carmella, hungering after a sister of her own. Mo held tight to the back of Dottie's jacket as they walked along.

"Then Al walked by. When he saw me, his eyes made exclamation points. Exclamation points are for, like, 'Oh, No!' or 'Dang!' He told me follow him."

Mo scanned the sidewalk, but by now Al had scurried out of sight.

Dottie wiped her runny nose on Mo's sleeve. "Don't tell Daddy, okay?"

Mo swallowed. "Don't worry."

Back home, Handsome's skin had shrunk against his toothpick bones, and his eyes goggled from his head. The instant they lifted the cover off his tank, he leaped up onto his rock, desperate as a castaway who's spied the rescue ship.

"Careful," said Mo. "He's fast."

Dottie dumped in two crickets. *Chirp!* sang the poor unsuspecting things. Handsome raised his front leg and held it motionless. His magnificent tail waved slowly from side to side. And then, the lunge! *Zap!* All that was left of the bugs were a few threadlike legs dangling from his jubilant jaw.

"H.W.," Dottie said softly. "You the man."

"Mo?" Mr. Wren called down from upstairs. "Where have you two been?"

Mo and Dottie's eyes locked in silent, sisterly agreement. But to their surprise, Mr. Wren didn't look angry. He sat in the armchair, shoe off, massaging his toe.

"You okay, Daddy?" Dottie asked.

"A guy once told me all my brains were in my big toe. I sure proved him wrong."

Mo indulged a sigh. He'd never know that she'd lost Dottie. That relief lasted two heartbeats.

"Mercedes called," he said next. "But don't worry."

Why was it that the second you heard certain phrases, you wanted to do the opposite? Don't laugh. Don't tell a soul. Don't look now.

Don't worry.

"Don't worry," he repeated. "I'll take you to Fox Street first thing in the morning."

The Return

Mr. Wren stopped the car on the corner of Fox and Paradise.

"I asked Cornelius if I could help with the move," he said. Cornelius C. Cunningham was Mercedes's stepfather's full name, though Mercedes preferred Three-C. "But he said Da's leaving most of her stuff behind. I guess that mini-mansion of theirs has everything she needs."

Mr. Wren rolled down his window and gazed at their old street.

"I'll keep my appointments," he said at last. By now Mo had given up asking him about his many appointments. He never told her anything anyway. "I'll be back early afternoon. That'll give me time to visit with Da before she goes."

"Okay." Mo climbed out of the car. Her father waved, rolled up his window, and pulled out onto Paradise.

Each time Mo had pictured this moment—and she'd lost count of how many times that was—she'd imagined herself running as fast as she could. So fast she was flying, really, an arrow winging straight for the heart of the street.

But now, just like in a dream, the ground got sticky. The best she could do was plod, past the Tip Top Club, silent this time of day, and the old Kowalski house, a FOR RENT sign stuck to the porch. Across the street, through the Baggotts' front window, she saw their TV flickering behind the cockeyed blinds. Saturday-morning cartoons.

Where was Pi? He didn't have any idea she was coming. Their paths could cross at any unexpected moment. Mo's heart crouched inside her, like someone at a surprise party waiting to jump out and yell.

A taken-apart lawn mower sprawled across Mr. Duong's porch. Mo inched along to Mrs. Steinbott's house. Her old neighbor cleaned house from floor to ceiling every Saturday. She shook rugs, scoured tile, attacked bedding—it was like living next door to a battle scene. But this morning no vacuum roared. The rosebushes, swaddled in burlap, looked spooky. Saturdays, Mrs. Steinbott boiled her sponges and hung them on the back line. Mo knew they'd be there, no matter what. Sidling around the far corner of the house, she peeked into the yard. The wash line was empty, except for a sparrow that flew away the instant it saw Mo.

Confused, Mo stumbled back out to the sidewalk. *Toot toot!* A big silver car pulled up.

"Mo!" The passenger door sprang open. "Maureen Jewel Wren!"

"Merce! Mercedes Jasmine Walcott!"

Mercedes had always been taller than Mo, and she hadn't quit growing. Since last summer, her long, straight bones had kept at it, and she bounded toward Mo like a golden-skinned gazelle.

A gazelle in a little fake-fur jacket.

They threw their arms around each other, then stepped back.

"You grew your hair!"

"So did you!"

"We're on Fox Street!"

"Together!"

"In winter!"

"I never even saw you wear a coat before!"

And then, because they were best friends, friends who shared everything from initials to brain waves, they were both struck speechless.

This is the last time.

"Ahem." Mercedes's stepfather was tall and handsome, the kind of man who wears hard, shiny shoes on Saturday. "It's a pleasure to see you, Mo."

Mo was immediately aware of the ketchup stain on her jacket. Not that he seemed to notice it. Instead, he reached into the car and hefted two big paper bags.

"We just made a Tortilla Feliz run. I believe there's a burro burrito in here with your name on it. "

Mo's favorite in all the world.

"Come inside," said Mercedes. "Everyone's dying to see you."

"But wait. Where's Mrs. Steinbott? Her sponges aren't out!"

"She joined a garden club, and they left early this morning on a bus trip to some orchid exhibit. We all said good-bye to her last night."

Mo pictured Mrs. Steinbott on a bus, talking to other old ladies about garden tools and bug poison. It made her smile.

"She promised to come visit us once the baby's born," said Three-C. At the mention of the baby, he hooked a finger inside his collar.

There were Da's metal porch chairs, with the backs shaped like seashells. The splintery porch floor, with the gaps between the boards. Inside, Da's house looked just the same too, except for the few suitcases and boxes beside the door. Mercedes and her parents had driven in yesterday, collected Da from rehab, and spent last night packing. As it turned out, the Walcott-Cunninghams were closing the house without putting it up for sale. At least not right away. Now that Da had finally agreed to come live with them, they weren't giving her time for second thoughts. They were hustling her straight down to Cincinnati.

In the hallway Mercedes shrugged off her fake-fur jacket. In her snug-fitting clothes, she looked more than ever like a long-legged gazelle.

A gazelle with a bra.

"That's a cute sweatshirt," she told Mo, touching the little embroidered bird.

"Thanks. I got it . . ." But Mo broke off. Saying she'd

gotten it from a lost and found would require a long story. She'd have to explain Carmella, and her idea about the world being a revolving door, and nothing ever really being lost. Ideas that made perfect sense when you were sitting in the Soap Opera but seemed strange here in Da's front hall. For the first time since they'd met, Mo felt shy with Mercedes.

"A friend gave it to me," Mo said.

"That's nice." Mercedes fingered one of her little gold earrings. Earrings! She'd gotten her ears pierced. "My friend gave me these," she said.

"Did it hurt?" Mo asked.

Mercedes looked confused. "Getting a present?"

"No, having your ears—"

"M and M!" called Three-C from the kitchen. "Your food's getting cold!"

"He drives me insane!" Mercedes said. "Wait'll you see how he hovers over Monette. You'd think she was a bomb set to go off any second."

Mercedes rubbed her nose. She possessed an ultra-sensitive sense of smell, like X-ray vision, only in her nose.

"It smells so sad in here," she said.

Now Mo smelled it too. A heavy blanket of mustiness hung over everything.

"I'm so glad she's coming with us," Mercedes said. "We're going to take the best care of her and . . ." She rubbed her nose again, tormented by the sad smell. "Last night, people kept coming over to say good-bye, one after the other. I've never been to a funeral, but that's what it felt like. I know they meant well, but it was pretty hard on Da."

Mo nodded. "That's how it was when we left."

"In her heart of hearts," Mercedes said, "she still doesn't want to come."

"Girls?" It was Monette's voice. "Is that my Mo Wren I hear out there?"

"Coming!" Mercedes called back but still didn't move. "She'll be happy with us. First she'll stay in our downstairs bedroom. But soon as she's strong again, she'll move upstairs into the guest suite. It has its own bathroom, plus it's right next door to my room."

"Your house is really big, isn't it?"

"Crazy big." Mercedes fiddled with her earring. "You're going to come stay with us this summer. You know that, right? Promise. Swear."

"Girls!" Monette's voice meant business now.

Da's dining-room ceiling hadn't been repaired, so they'd all crowded around the kitchen table. Da wore her good Sunday pants suit and her pearl earrings.

Her arm was in a sling. Her face was thin and drawn, and when she saw Mo, her head trembled on its long neck.

"Give me strength. How are you, child?"

"I'm all right, Da. How are you?" She looked so frail, Mo was afraid to hug her.

"I've been better." Her free hand went to her cheek. "Thank heaven you sold your house to Sarah and Tim. They've been so good to me—and that baby! She's so naughty, now and then I slip and call her Dottie. They came over last night to say good-bye, and promise to keep an eye on the house, and . . ."

Her voice trailed off. Everyone looked uncomfortable, till Monette threw out her arms.

"Mo! Give me a hug, my other daughter!"

Monette was tall and slender, just like Mercedes and Da. But when she swiveled away from the table, Mo gasped. Nestled in her lap, beneath her pretty, gauzy shirt, was one big mound of baby. Monette laughed.

"As if you've never seen a pregnant mama! You're the only one here who's a big sister!" Monette caught Mo's hand. "Someone's telling me he wants to meet you."

Gently she pressed Mo's hand to her belly. A baby

dolphin rolled and dove beneath Mo's fingers, then all at once grew legs and kicked her.

"It karate'd me!"

"Are we going to have our hands full with this one, or *what*!" Monette's voice was too loud and mega bright, a TV-commercial voice. Her eyes slid in Da's direction. "Good thing I've got help on the way!"

Three-C was heaping everyone's plate with food.

"Eat, Ma," urged Monette. "You've got to gain your weight back."

Casually, as if he did it every day, Three-C reached over and cut Da's tortilla into bite-size pieces. Da looked away.

"Oh!" Monette's hand flew to her belly.

"Are you all right?" Three-C leaped to his feet.

"Just an especially hard kick."

"Do you want a pillow? Your special tea? Maybe you should lie down."

Mercedes threw Mo a see-what-I-mean? look. But Mo was having a hard time paying attention to anything besides Da, who hadn't eaten a bite. Mercedes was right. It wasn't just kids and lizards who got dragged places they didn't really want to go.

Now nobody could think of a word to say. Da rested her cheek on her good hand. Elbows on the table!

Normally, she'd swat anyone who did it. Three-C, a man accustomed to being in charge of all he surveyed, fiddled helplessly with his napkin. Monette's cheeriness dimmed like the lights at the Wren House, as if staying bright was just too hard.

"Ma, I know this is tearing you up," she said. "But we can't be worrying about you like we have. It's not only for you—it's for the whole family's sake."

For the whole family's sake. Mr. Wren had said the same kind of thing over and over, when they moved. Mind reader that she was, Da fixed her gaze on Mo.

"What do you have to say, faithful scout?"

All eyes turned to her. Mo wanted to help, more than anything. But she never lied to Da. What could she say that would be true yet still help? Everybody waited, squished tight and anxious around the little table. They made Mo think of that big green armchair, squeezed into the Wrens' upstairs hallway. She'd been so sure her heart would break if they left it behind, but taking it had turned out to be a mistake. Sometimes the chair itself looked miserable, with everyone bumping shins and stubbing toes against it. It looked as if it knew it didn't belong there.

"Nothing worthwhile is easy, right, Da? That's what you always told us."

"You always were my star pupil." Da gave a half smile. "Go on."

"Leaving's really hard. But if you really love some-place, it kind of comes along with you, wherever you go. Like the moon. You can't touch it, but when you look for it, it's there."

Monette flashed Mo a grateful look, then turned to her mother.

"Oh, Ma," she said, eyes shining. "Just think of it. Once you come, three generations of us will live together under one roof. What does it matter whose roof it is?"

Da curled her fingers around Mo's. And then, at last, she began to eat.

Soon Three-C and Monette began hinting how it was a long five-hour trip, and why drive in the dark and . . . Next thing you knew, the dishes were done, the heat was turned down, and Mo and Mercedes were helping carry Da's things out to the car.

"Thanks for what you said," Three-C told Mo. "Life's all about risk. Just between you and me"—he lowered his voice, pretending he didn't want Mercedes to hear—"I was scared to death to become a stepfather. But give me strength!" He grinned. "When I think of what I might have missed."

Mercedes threw her hands over her eyes. "Spare me!"

"There are many wonderful, exceptional things about Mercedes," Three-C went on, "including the fact that she came ready-made. This new baby. on the other hand . . ." He gulped.

Monette was helping Da down the front steps. It was earlier than expected, and Mr. Wren was going to miss saying good-bye.

"We'll give you a ride home," said Three-C.

"My father's coming," Mo said.

"Here, better call him." He handed Mo his phone.

But her father didn't answer. Maybe he was in the middle of one of his important appointments, or maybe he was already on his way. Mo knew the Walcotts wanted to get going, and why give them one more thing to worry about?

"Any minute now?" she said into the phone. "Okay, I'll be waiting right on Da's porch." Handing back the phone, she said, "He's really sorry he won't get to see you, but he sends all his best."

At the bottom of her front steps, Da paused beside

the big lilac bush. Who knew how old it was? It had always been there, busy with blossoms and honeybees each spring, shading the porch with its heart-shaped leaves all summer. Mo watched her break off a twig and slip it into her coat pocket. Would she keep it in the drawer of her new dresser?

Unhooking her arm from Monette's, Da lifted her chin and walked the rest of the way to the car by herself. The one-armed hug she gave Mo was stiff and quick. Mo could tell she didn't trust herself to linger a moment longer. When Three-C opened the car door, Mo got a glimpse of leather seats, cushy with pillows and blankets.

"We didn't even get to talk!" said Mercedes. "I love your hair long."

"You do?"

"It's like you're the same, but different."

"I am?"

Mercedes's stepfather started the car, and she made a face. "He's in such a hurry, let him leave without me."

"He's not so bad."

"I know." Mercedes hugged Mo, and her nose did an accordion imitation. "Umm! You using some new kind of laundry soap? You smell so good." Stepping back, she grinned. "Oh, Mo, I'm so happy! You are too, right? Remember you promised to come this summer! We'll start a countdown, okay?"

She climbed into the car. A toot of the horn, a wave of hands. Mo watched the silver car roll up Fox Street and disappear.

The Plum Tree

Mo sat on Da's porch, waiting for her father.

Mrs. Petrone drove by, her hair swept up high and wearing her good black coat, which meant she was on her way to her job at the funeral home. Down at Mr. Duong's, the lawn mower he was fixing roared and sputtered and died. An upstairs window at the Baggotts' rattled upward and a pillow flew out, *flump*-ing to the grass. Someone shouted, and the window slammed shut again.

It was chilly on the porch, out of the sun. Behind her, Da's house sighed, settling its bones.

Across the street, you could hardly see the grass

for all the bright plastic toys strewn around. The new front door had four square windows instead of a single round one. In the driveway, that rusty beater of a car basked in the sun like it was entitled to be there.

The side door opened. Out they came, Sarah and Tim in coats that had seen better days. But Min wore a fat new jacket that turned her into a marshmallow with a head. The door swung closed neatly, without a sound. Mo slid down in her chair. Sarah held Min in her arms, but the baby squirmed and pitched herself forward till her mother set her down. Arms out like a miniature plane, she propelled herself forward. The tassels on her hat spun and swayed. Min could walk! Sort of. Seconds later she was down, *oof.* Instead of crying, she picked something off the ground and popped it in her mouth.

Peering between the porch rails, Mo watched Tim fish it back out.

"Baa baa!" he said, then "Ouch! No biting!" Meanwhile, Sarah fetched the stroller, and before she knew it, Min was buckled up and speeding toward Paradise. Tim started singing that song about baby whales. His voice was strong and true.

Mo waited till they were out of sight, and then she waited a little longer, making sure the coast was clear.

Looking both ways, she darted across Fox Street and up her old driveway.

The plum tree was like an ink drawing, all stark black lines, but Mo wasn't fooled. She knew that tree. She could see how the tips of its branches had begun to swell. New life, all excited and eager, pulsed inside it. "Here we go," that tree was saying. "Get ready for some blossoms!"

A tipped-over yellow plastic pail lay beneath it. Shriveled-up plums from last year spilled out onto the ground. Min must collect them, the way Dottie used to. Mo picked one up, thinking she'd tuck it into her pocket, but it squished in her hand, all used up.

"There's a tree by my new house." Mo hooked an arm around the tree's trunk. "Nowhere near as good as you." She leaned her cheek against the rough bark. "It's really scrawny." And then, just as if the plum tree had replied, Mo had a new thought. "Probably because it practically grows out of the sidewalk cement. How does it do that, anyway?"

Overhead, the top branches swayed and dipped, saying, "That's how trees are, Mo Wren. We do our best, wherever we're planted."

A vine of tenderness climbed up inside Mo. In some rooty, steadfast way, the two trees were related.

She sat down, fitting her backbone against the trunk, waiting to be comfortable. But the ground was cold, and her father would show up any minute, and who knew when Min and her family would come back? Long before she felt ready, Mo stood up. Crossing the grass, she gave one tire of their car a kick.

A familiar clatter made her whirl around. Out in the street, arms at his side, long hair lifting like curtains in the breeze, Pi coasted by on his skateboard.

The Red Sweatshirt

Mo's hands flew to her own hair, smoothing it back. She ran down the driveway and waved. Pi gave a shout and swerved.

"Mo!" He pulled up.

Another skater sailed by. A girl, about Mo's age.

"Whoa!" Pi flipped his board and caught it in both hands. He stared at Mo. "What are you doing here?"

"Hello to you too," she said.

The girl, who wore a million layers of clothes and a striped knit cap pulled low, pivoted.

"That's Clara," said Pi as she rolled by again without stopping. "She lives over there." He waved a hand in the direction of Paradise. "She still can't do a one-eighty, but she's getting close."

"Wow," said Mo. "Impressive. Did you teach her?"

"Huh?" Pi set his skateboard down. "Clara? She taught herself." He pinched his bottom lip. Those lips were still the softest thing in his bony face. "I didn't know you were coming."

"I had to say good-bye to Da."

"Oh yeah. We all said good-bye last night."

Clara coasted by again. She wore knee pads over her washed-out jeans. Her high-tops were checkered. Mo had never seen her before, but something about her looked familiar.

"I sent you a letter," Pi said.

At the thought of that letter, and how happy it had made her, Mo felt her foolish cheeks heat up. All this time she'd been imagining him missing her! Dragging his feet as he slumped past her house. While instead he'd been blissfully skateboarding with Clara. Here she came again, crouched down, concentrating.

"That day I found your shirt in the driveway, all soggy and dirty with tire tracks on it . . ." Pi shook his shaggy head.

It was Mo's turn to stare at him. "What?"

"And then every time I walked past your house . . ."

Clara rolled to a stop beside them. "You coming, man?" she asked.

"This is Mo. She used to live on Fox Street."

Clara had freckles and a big, toothy smile. She was the kind of girl Mo might like, under different circumstances. Including if she wasn't wearing Mo's sweatshirt.

"Hey!" said Mo. "What are you doing with my shirt?"

Startled, Clara looked down at herself.

"I almost forgot!" said Pi. "That's Mo's sweatshirt."

Clara unzipped her down vest. Underneath, sure enough, there it was. Clara tugged it over her head. She still wore a thermal shirt and a T-shirt.

"How . . . what are you doing with it?" Mo asked.

"Like, one day we were skating and I tried this half-pipe and wiped out and got a big rip in my shirt and Pi said like, hang on, and he went inside his house and . . ." Clara held it out. "Thanks for the loan, man. It's still pretty clean."

Mo shoved her hands into her pockets. "Never mind," she said. "You keep it."

"But . . . I washed it and everything. I even got the

tire tracks out." Pi held it up so she could see. Confusion and disappointment whittled his face even sharper. "Clara was just borrowing it. I told her you wouldn't mind."

"I got a new one." Mo pointed to her lost and found shirt. "I don't need it anymore." She tucked her hands in her armpits to keep from changing her mind and grabbing it. "She can . . . You can keep it, Clara."

"Cool," said Clara. "Thanks."

"You're welcome. Man."

Clara knotted the shirt around her waist, pulled her cap back down, and pushed off. "I'm going to the parking garage. You coming?"

"Yeah." Pi turned to Mo. "You staying?"

"My dad's picking me up any minute."

Pi traced a gentle half circle around her.

"It's good you're good, Mo," he said.

Her heart did that little sparkler imitation.

"Okay." He set his foot down and pushed off. The sparkler had nearly fizzled out when he arced back around. "Are you going to visit again?"

"I don't know."

"All right then. Bye."

"Bye."

The clatter of his board faded in the distance. Mo looked around. For the first time in her life, she felt lonesome on Fox Street.

She started walking toward the corner.

Passengers

Up on Paradise Avenue, Mo watched one car after another go by. At the pay phone outside the Tip Top Club, she tried calling her father again. Something must have happened. Her father forgot a lot of things, but not her. He never, ever forgot Mo.

At the bus shelter on the next corner, a curly-haired woman held a big brown portfolio on her lap. A fuzzy bit of yellow poked out from inside her open jacket.

"Does the crosstown bus stop here?" Mo asked her.

"The number eighteen. And your timing is perfect—here it comes. You have exact change?"

"Oh, no."

"Hang on." She dug in the pocket of her jeans. "Here you go," she said, spilling quarters into Mo's palm. When Mo thanked her, she just smiled and asked, "What stop do you want?"

"Umm, by Eastside Park?"

"Me too!"

As they boarded the bus, Mo took a closer look at her yellow sweater. It was new, not baggy at all, and its buttons were black, not pearls.

Never in her life had Mo been alone on a public bus. She gazed out the smudged window. Riding a bus set you high above things, making it all a little unreal, like watching a movie. When the bus turned onto the bridge, she saw how the steely blue of the lake met the more fragile blue of the late-day sky, two blocks of color coming to rest against each other.

"Isn't it beautiful?" the curly-haired woman asked from across the aisle.

"Yeah."

"I love traveling, even on a grotty old city bus!"

The bus bumped along, stopping and starting. At last Mo saw the park.

When they got off, the woman in the yellow sweater waved and hurried away.

"I'm back," Mo told the faithful bus shelter.

She almost wished she'd stayed on the bus. Being in motion, being a traveler, you weren't here and you weren't there. Life stayed at a distance.

But now she was back. And life came rushing at her.

What happened? Where is he?

She broke into a run.

The Curse, Part Three

The way Dottie was howling and carrying on—Mo had never seen her sister behave that way. Not even when their mother died. Then she'd been too little to really understand.

"What? What's wrong?"

"Handsome!" Dottie was in a heap on the dining-room floor. Now she crawled over and grabbed her big sister by the ankles. "He's gone!"

"No!" How could it be? He'd looked just fine when Mo fed him his breakfast cricket before she left— today? Was that really just this morning?

"You mean he . . ." Mo couldn't make herself say *died.*

"He's nowhere!" Dottie rested her forehead on Mo's shoe. "We've been looking and looking and we can't find him."

Oh! That kind of gone. Now Mo noticed what an uproar the room was in. Chairs were shoved aside, glasses pulled off the shelves. A metal plate had been unscrewed from the wall, and darkness gaped behind it. Handsome's tank stood on the bar, lid off. She sat on the floor beside her sister.

"How'd he get out? What happened?"

"I was teaching him a new trick."

Though she could barely fit, Dottie climbed into Mo's lap. She made Mo remember trying to wedge into her mother's lap when she was so pregnant with Dottie, there was hardly any room. Mo had been determined to fit, making her mother laugh. No sooner did her mother pull that moonbeam curtain around her than suddenly, out of nowhere, Mo had felt a kick right in the head. She'd yelped, and her mother had chuckled. "This is going to be a wild one," she'd whispered, as if it was a secret between just her and Mo.

"I t-tried to hold on to him," Dottie stuttered.

"I tried to hold onnn . . ."

"Oh, no." Mr. Wren, flashlight in hand, froze in the doorway. He flattened his hand against his brow. "Oh, no."

"It's okay," said Mo. "I took the bus. I'm fine."

"Why'd he run away?" asked Dottie. Her voice was jagged, strewn with bits of broken heart. "I thought he liked it here."

"He did," Mr. Wren said. "I mean, he does! Handsome loves you. But sometimes . . . sometimes creatures just can't help themselves. They do stupid things."

When Dottie started crawling around again, he told Mo in a low voice, "I'm really sorry. I've been on lizard patrol for hours. I searched every heating duct, all over the basement . . . the guy just vanished." He shook his head. "He's the Corky of reptiles."

Mo looked at the empty tank with its crayoned decorations, its miniature palm tree and heat rock. The Wren House was so chilly, how could thin-skinned little Handsome survive? Not to mention if he'd somehow gotten outside, into the coldest winter on record. She tried not to think about how sad he looked when he missed a meal.

"Look!" Dottie picked up something from the floor. "His tail! He dropped his tail!"

It was a mess of bulging, fleshy stuff, like a tortilla oozy with raw meat. Mo was not the squeamish kind. But a very bad taste rose in the back of her mouth.

"Now he'll get infected," Dottie said. "Carmella's book says you have to put medicine on them when this happens, or they get infected!"

"But it happens in the wild, right?" Mo struggled to sound convincing. "And they don't get medicine then. So maybe . . ." She looked to Mr. Wren for help.

"Handsome's a tough guy," he said. "Hey, how about some supper, what do you say? Dottie's Delight coming up, huh?"

But Dottie just rolled her meatballs around her plate without taking a bite. Mo sighed. It was the second time today she'd shared a table with a person who had lost her appetite.

"Some girl called here," Mr. Wren told Mo. "She said you were supposed to go shopping with her today. I told her you don't like shopping, but she insisted."

"Megan! Oh, no! I forgot all about her!"

Mo found the slip of paper with Megan's phone number and called. When Mo said how sorry she was, Megan made a sniffing sound. Maybe, Mo told her, maybe they could go shopping another day.

"Tomorrow I have a birthday party," Megan said.

"My mother works during the week, and my baby-sitter would never take us."

"Maybe my father could drop us off," Mo said.

"Drop us off!" Megan's voice was as horrified as if Mo had suggested swimming among crocodiles. "My mother never permits me to get dropped off. The world is full of perverts."

"Well," said Mo, "maybe we can do it another time. I hope."

"Maybe," said Megan, and hung up.

Mo looked at her reflection in the mirror over the bar. Her face was too long, and her hair was scragglier than ever. She pushed a lock behind her ear, remembering how Mercedes said she liked it. Probably she was just trying to think of something nice to say. Mercedes with her pierced ears and fake-fur jacket. And bra. Turning sideways, Mo ran a hand down her own same old uneventful front. She pictured Clara in her little knit cap and cool, checkered high-tops. Like an itch she couldn't reach, discontent took hold of Mo. Nothing was right anymore. Not even her own face in the mirror.

Dottie was asleep with her head on the table. When Mr. Wren picked her up, she came awake long enough to say, "It's the curse."

"Uh-huh, sure." He carried her upstairs, her feet knocking against his thighs. Mo darted ahead, pushing the green chair out of the way.

"Put her in my bed," she said.

Mr. Wren pulled off Dottie's socks and shoes and settled her under the covers.

"Look how big she's getting," he said softly. "One of these days she's not going to fit in your bed anymore."

Dottie rolled over, kicking off her covers. "The curse," she muttered. "Corky's curse!"

"What's she been watching?" Mr. Wren frowned, covering her back up. He sat down heavily and picked at a splotch of dried mustard on his knee.

Uh-oh. Mo had read that Eskimos have over a hundred different ways to say "snow." What about the Wrens and "uh-oh"?

"This isn't the best day in Wren history." Mr. Wren kept working at the mustard. "I didn't get the loan, Mo. Small-business loans are almost impossible to score right now, and I don't have the credit history they want."

"That's stupid! Try another bank, Daddy."

"Five. I tried five, Mojo." Mr. Wren flicked his fingers. "The decision's unanimous."

Mo's room, usually too cold, felt stuffy, as if all its air was secondhand.

"You were right," he went on. "I need to hire help, but there is no way I can afford it now. Me and Handsome. We both lost our tails today." Setting his hands on his knees, Mr. Wren pushed himself up so slowly, you could almost hear him creak. "I've got to figure out how to grow a new one, I guess." He pulled the covers back over Dottie once again, then rumpled Mo's hair. "You get to sleep now too."

When he was gone, Mo flattened her palms against the stuck window, bent her knees, and pushed upward with all her might. If nothing else, she'd open this dumb window and let some fresh air in! But it refused to budge. The stubborn, ancient caked paint held fast.

Swimming across the Ocean

Dottie was in a booth crayoning signs that said *last lizerd, big rewad!!!!!* when Shawn showed up to ask why they hadn't been to the Soap Opera. As Mo explained about Handsome, he nodded.

"I used to have this black cat," he said. "He was like a mini-panther. Every morning he jumped on my bed. *Hellllo?* he'd say." Shawn turned his voice into a cross between a cat's and a human's. *"Hellllo?"*

Dottie didn't crack a smile. She was waiting for the end of the story.

"He was a big thug. One of his ears had this really cool notch in it, from fighting." Shawn rubbed his eyes and turned away. "It's awfully dusty in here."

"So?" Dottie asked. "Where is he?"

"He got run over."

You'd think a person would run out of tears after a while. But Dottie cried so rarely, she must have stored up an endless supply. Shawn whacked himself in the forehead.

"Hey. Yo, Dot, guess what? One of these days I'm going to go around the world, and you know why?"

"Why?" she wept.

"Because you can't go through it!"

Dottie made a snorkeling sound.

"Look." He reached into his backpack. "I got a new book, like you recommended." He held it up.

"Miseries of the Universe," Dottie read.

"Mysteries! For example, how stars run out of fuel and blow up and get pulverized till all that's left is a little ball of matter so heavy, one teaspoon weighs a million tons."

Dottie wiped her eyes, and Shawn, encouraged, said, "I know! We can put up a lost lizard notice at Carmella's. Everybody reads that bulletin board."

"You're nice," said Dottie.

Mo reached for her blue sweatshirt. The weather was turning too warm for it, but still she kept on wearing it. No longer did she worry that someone else might come looking for it. It belonged to her now.

At the Soap Opera, Homer was out front, cleaning up mushy, snow-flattened trash. Inside, Dottie marched up to Carmella, reached into her pocket, and held out her hand. Handsome's shriveled-up tail, stuck with bits of pocket fuzz, lay on her palm like something out of a nightmare.

Carmella pressed a hand to her heart. "Good lord."

"When they drop their tail, it wiggles all around like it's still alive." Dottie touched the inert tail. "To trick the creditor."

"Predator," said Mo. "She means . . ."

"I get it," said Carmella. "Hold on, sugar."

She hurried to the lost and found and returned with a big plaid handkerchief. Looking solemn, she wrapped the tail, then set it inside an empty dryer-sheet box.

"Now the ground's thawing, you can give it a proper burial," she told Dottie.

As Shawn helped Dottie pin up the LOST notice, Carmella put her hands on her hips and turned to Mo.

"Does your daddy know she's carrying that thing around in her pocket?"

"He's been sort of distracted lately," Mo said.

"Hmm." Disapproving was too mild a word for the look on Carmella's face. "Too distracted to mind his baby girl?"

"We're in big trouble. The banks turned us down. Five banks! He was counting on a loan."

There it was, the truth blurted out in one big, ugly blob. Mo hadn't meant to tell a soul. But she couldn't have Carmella getting the wrong idea about her father.

"I don't know what happened to all the rest of the money." Mo swallowed. "But if things don't turn around soon, I don't know. I don't know if we're going to make it."

"This reminds me of the woman who tried to swim across the ocean." Carmella folded her arms on her chest. "She got halfway, then decided she was too tired and swam on back."

"That doesn't make any sense."

"Exactly." Carmella tapped her foot. "You Wrens can't turn back now."

Homer came inside. Wiping his hands on a towel, he read Dottie's notice.

"What the big rewad?" he asked.

"A lifetime of free meals at the Wren House," Dottie told him.

"The Wren House? Never heard of it."

"The sign still says Corky's."

"Oh," said Homer. "That place."

Carmella stopped tapping her foot and drew Mo over to Number Three. "Remember the day we fixed this?" She patted the machine, running smooth as could be. "Who was helping me when you got here?"

"Homer."

Carmella nodded, that light in her eyes growing brighter.

"He knows how to do some of everything, from plumbing to electrical. Once he had his own big dream. He meant to run a contracting business. Homes by Homer. But then he hit a skid of rotten luck. He got sick, he lost his job, his girl ditched him, and somehow he never got back on his feet."

Homer had settled into his customary seat by the door. It was difficult to imagine the man Carmella described, bustling with plans and ambition.

"He's one of those folk who got done in and never got back out. I'm glad he feels at home here. And on his good days, he's no end of help to me. But I've been trying to think how to help ease him out into the world."

By now her eyes were practically twin lighthouses.

"How'd you like a helper?"

"What?" said Mo.

"Believe me, he'd be a huge help. And your father could just pay him minimum wage, for now. And some of that cooking you keep bragging on. Good home cooking, that's one thing I can't give Homer." She laughed, showing her crooked teeth. "What do you say, sugar? Think your distracted daddy will consider it?"

It wasn't really a question. Or at least, with those eyes on you, there was only one answer.

Free to a Good Home

Late Sunday morning, the last day of vacation, Carmella and Homer came to the Wren House. She wore her church clothes, a swirly pink dress and high heels, topped off with a little purple hat that fitted close to her head. Definitely not a lost and found outfit.

Mr. Wren was in the middle of knocking out the wall between the two bathrooms. Wiping his gritty palm on his jeans, he shook Homer's hand.

"And you're Carmella." Mr. Wren wiped his hand again, making extra sure it was clean before he took Carmella's.

Mr. Wren showed Homer the pile of rubble that was supposed to turn into a bathroom. Instead of two small rooms, he explained, they needed one big handicapped-accessible one. Homer listened, tapping walls, bending to examine the exposed pipes.

"Galvanized steel plumbing," he said. "Long time since I saw that."

"Look how rusted out the fittings are," said Mr. Wren.

"You got a socket wrench?"

Carmella gave Mo the thumbs-up. "I think this is going to work." She hurried away to open the Soap Opera.

When suppertime rolled around, Homer and Mr. Wren were still working. Mo got out the biscuit mix and stirred up a batch. After she'd popped the tray in the oven, she took the pot of leftover pea soup from the refrigerator and set it on a burner. Squaring her shoulders, ordering herself, Stay calm!, she grasped the stove's finicky knob. By now she'd memorized just how far her father pushed it in before giving it a quick flick to the right. The gas flames leaped up! But when she pressed and twisted the knob, they obediently sank low.

"Yes!" She was master of the stove. Mo added a little

broth to the soup, and some bits of leftover ham. Back in the dining room, she set a booth with four places and poured glasses of milk.

"Come and get it!" she called.

Mr. Wren stared at the steaming bowls of soup and the basket of hot biscuits.

"Where'd all this come from?"

"Who cares?" said Homer, sitting down. He spooned up soup, giving a contented grunt between bites. "Sit down."

Her father picked up his spoon and laid it back down. Mo decided to get a jump on his lecture.

"You were here, so it's not disobeying. Go on, taste it."

He did. "Too salty, as usual. I got a lead foot with that saltshaker."

"I know how to fix that," Mo said. "You put a potato in. It absorbs the salt. I saw it at Carmella's on the cooking channel."

Homer was already wiping out his bowl with a biscuit. By the time Mo brought him back seconds, he was telling Mr. Wren what a difference a new breaker box would make. The furnace, though—he was worried about that knocking sound it made. Mr. Wren kept laying down his spoon to make notes.

"That's what Daddy needed," Dottie said later. Their father had left to drive Homer back to the shelter. "He needed a friend." She climbed the stairs in slow motion, eyes on the ground, on perpetual lookout for Handsome. "I wish it wasn't school tomorrow."

"But you love school. You haven't seen K.C. or anybody the whole vacation."

"What if he comes looking for me and I'm not here? What if he thinks I don't care about him anymore?" Head down, Dottie bumped into the green chair. "Ow," she said in a small voice.

Suddenly Mo had had enough of that chair.

"Let's surprise Daddy," she heard herself say. "Let's haul it out of here before he gets back."

You could always count on Dottie to love a surprise.

It was like moving a boulder. Halfway down the stairs they lost their grip, and the poor thing *bump-bump-bump*ed the rest of the way. Their father still hadn't shown up, thank goodness, as they wrangled it through the front door, or as Dottie made a sign that said FREE TO A GOOD HOM. He wasn't back yet when they each took one last turn sitting in it, out there on the sidewalk, or when they bade it a final good-bye and went inside.

By the time they heard him climbing the stairs,

they were already in their pajamas. They crouched in the doorway of Mo's room, spying. He was singing, for the first time in weeks. They watched him step into the hallway, then rear back, crying out as if he'd stubbed his toe after all.

"Surprise!" they yelled, jumping up.

"What? Where's my favorite instrument of torture?"

In the morning, Mo watched a sparrow perch on the curved arm of the chair and turn its head from side to side in astonishment at the big green shrub, sprung up overnight. Hopping onto the cushion, the bird pecked at the hole, then flew into the sidewalk tree, a bit of stuffing trailing from its beak.

A moment later, Homer rounded the corner, wearing a freshly washed pair of overalls.

Mo Wren, Murderer

Your hair looks cute in a ponytail.

The note slid onto Mo's desk, startling her. She'd been afraid it was all over between her and Megan.

Thanks, Mo wrote back. *How was your vacation?*

But before Megan could write back, Mr. Grimm did his clapping routine, and it was all eyes up front.

"It's spring," he said. "That means mud and baseball and cute new outfits, but best of all it means science fair! This year, we're going to mix things up. To encourage both exploration and collaboration, you'll work in teams. Before anyone asks, yes, you can pick your partners. But!" He tapped his forehead. "I want you to think! Don't automatically choose your friends. This is your chance to work with someone new. It's an opportunity to discover . . ."

Poor Mr. Grimm. Didn't he notice nobody heard a word after "You can pick your partners"? Mary and Asha were already signaling each other. Mo kept her own eyes on her desk. In his seat, Shawn began humming in that terrible monotone way.

"We'll sign up partners after lunch," said Mr. Grimm.

Megan slipped into line behind Mo. "I hate science. I wish it was still vacation." She bit her glossy lip. "Even though mine turned out to be a disaster."

"Me too. My sister's lizard escaped."

"Really?" Megan's pale face flushed pink and spotty, as if she'd come down with a sudden rash. "My goldfish died. I had Cutie for three years, practically since I was a baby! I wasn't going to tell anyone, because every time I talk about it . . ."

Her eyes widened, and a hiccup flew out of her mouth. Not just any hiccup, but the loudest, most violent hiccup Mo had ever witnessed. Followed by another, and then another.

"Megan, are you all right?" asked Mr. Grimm from the head of the line.

Megan shuddered as if she'd swallowed an earth-quake. Some kids started giggling. Asha rolled her eyes.

"Megan?" said Mr. Grimm. "Do you need to see the nurse?"

Megan, her face brilliant red, shook her head.

"I'll make sure she's okay," said Mo.

"You're a good citizen, Mo Wren," said their teacher.

Megan could hardly eat. By recess she was still hic-cupping, and Mo was getting worried. Just when it seemed as if she might be over it, Megan couldn't resist telling one more remarkable thing about Cutie. Cutie used to ripple his tail like a golden scarf when-ever he saw her. *Hiccup.* Cutie adored romaine lettuce. *Hic! Cup!*

Outside, they huddled by the fence, Mo rubbing her back.

"No big deal," Shawn informed them, pointing to his watch. "You've only been hiccupping for about forty minutes. The world record is sixty-eight years."

Megan ducked behind Mo. "Please make him go away."

"Her fish died," Mo whispered to Shawn. "She's really sad."

"Whoa." He balled his hands into fists and knocked

them together. "I'm sorry, Megan," he said. "That stinks. That stinks on a cosmic scale."

"I know. Thank you." Megan put her hands over her eyes. *Hiccup!*

A moment later, a roar like a lion crossed with a locomotive shattered the air. Megan shrieked and threw herself at Mo. Here it came again, louder yet.

"Stop!" Megan waved her arms at Shawn. "Now I have hiccups plus a heart attack!"

Shawn noted the time. Megan collapsed on a bench, her head in her hands. Mo kept rubbing her back, even though her hand was getting very tired. A hiccup-free moment passed. Then another.

"Two minutes and seven seconds," croaked Shawn, his voice hoarse from roaring.

At last Megan lifted her head. She looked at Mo and whispered, "I think it worked."

"Please, hold your applause." Shawn bowed.

"You're so weird, it's like a talent." Megan picked at her chapped lip. "Mary and Asha will think I'm super-terminal weird, hiccupping my head off like that."

"Probably," said Shawn. "But the science of hiccups would be an excellent project. Or else I was thinking black holes. You know, the devouring monsters of the universe?"

Megan's head drooped. She twirled a strand of pale hair. "You two are going to be partners, right?"

Shawn craned his neck and hummed. Mo massaged her sore hand.

"You should," Megan told her. "I take back the bad stuff I said about him."

"Mr. Grimm didn't say it could only be two people," Mo said.

"Cool!" Shawn went for the invisible dunk. "I have my tutor today—I'll ask her can I start researching right away. Tomorrow the three of us can have a conference."

Megan blinked her blue eyes. Little coins of pink prettied up her pale cheeks. As they lined up to go back in, Mr. Grimm asked her if she was all right now.

"I'm good," she said.

"Thanks to a certain someone's talent," said Shawn.

"A really humble someone," said Mo.

For once Mo was grateful Dottie had an after-school invitation. What with Megan and Cutie, she couldn't really handle any more pet sadness today. And after a week of no hot rock and no crickets, it was hard to keep reassuring Dottie that Handsome was all right.

But when school let out, Mo found her sister waiting for her.

"K.C. and I are in a fight," she said.

"What happened?"

"She said it's my fault Handsome got away. She said it was dumb to try to teach him a trick. I said no, it wasn't. She said lizards can't learn things. I said maybe some can't, but Handsome can. She said I'm not new anymore, so why do I think I'm so special? I said—"

"Okay, okay. I get the idea."

"She says she's not my BFF anymore. What's a BFF?"

"Big fat foofoo."

As they approached the pigeon-feeders' bench, the men lowered their binoculars. Their apple-cheeked faces creased into kindly smiles.

"Young miss," said one, "you look so sad. Would you like to feed a pigeon?"

"No, thank you," said Dottie. "My father says they're flying rats."

They walked on, but after a moment Dottie ran back.

"While you look for birds, could you keep an eye out for a lizard? He has no tail, and his head is covered with spots. He might have a bug hanging out of his mouth."

The men looked at each other.

"Very concise description," said one.

"I'm sure we'll recognize him if he comes by," said the other.

"Bring him to the Wren House," Dottie said. "There's a big reward."

A baby rode by in his stroller, kicking his heels as if to make it go faster, and every swing had a little kid on it. All around the empty wading pool, leaves shaped like butter knives poked up through the dirt. A boy with his arm around a girl inscribed their names on the wall of the bus shelter. Suddenly, Dottie skidded to a halt.

"The Wren House!" she said. "How are they going to find the Wren House when the sign still says Corky's?"

With all the projects Mr. Wren had done, he'd never taken down that sign.

The green chair was gone. A rock under the tree anchored the FREE TO A GOOD HOM notice. On the back, someone had penciled MUCHAS GRACIAS. Mo and Dottie lugged out an aluminum ladder, and Dottie held it steady as Mo clambered up. From the top she had a perfect view of the sparrow nest. It was messy, made up of bits of this and that. No eggs yet. What was that white fluff waving in the breeze? Mo leaned a little closer. Armchair stuffing! Reinvented as part of a baby bird cradle.

The CORKY'S sign hung from a bent metal bar. The chains holding it were rusty, but when Mo tugged on the links, they held fast. Beat up as it was, that sign was not letting go.

"Keep trying," said Dottie.

Mo noticed the gaps in the topmost links, where the chain hooked onto the bar, and started wiggling first one, then the other. The stubborn metal bit her fingers, turning them rusty orange. She worked the links up and down and sideways, like some monster puzzle. Her foot skidded sideways on the rung, and she grabbed the ladder to keep from falling.

"Careful!" called Dottie. "Come on, sign! You might as well just give up!"

Mo gave another yank. *Whoosh*. One corner came loose and swayed outward, then swung back to crash against the ladder. *Clang!* The collision of metal against metal sent shudders through Mo's arms and legs. A moment later, the opposite corner came loose.

"Timber!" yelled Dottie as the sign hit the sidewalk.

She picked it up and marched around to the alley, where she hurled it into a trash can and dusted her hands together. "That's that! R.I.P.!"

Mo flexed her sore fingers. She felt a little dizzy. Maybe it was being up so high. But maybe it was realizing what she'd just done. Corky's was dead, and she was the murderer.

Inches from Mo's face, the empty sign holder gave her an accusing look. "Okay, you win," it seemed to say. "Now what?"

No Turning Back

After that, things really speeded up.

Homer came nearly every day. Sometimes he left abruptly, without an explanation. Sometimes he didn't leave but didn't work either, instead taking a nap in a booth, or sitting with Dottie at the bar, watching TV. But nearly every afternoon, Mo discovered something newly done. The bathroom was framed out and drywalled. The lights burned steady. One night when Mo went to start the stove, she discovered a shiny knob that turned without any coaxing.

"This is how the most important things in life happen." Her father set a just-delivered stack of aprons and bar rags on a shelf. "Like making a friend. Or learning how to throw a curveball. It's gradual, then all of a sudden."

Mr. Wren bought new knives. A new deluxe blender for the bar. He had his favorite sports posters framed, and he and Mo hung them all around the Moonglow walls.

Mo was pretty sure her father was spending every penny they had left. And maybe some they didn't have. Going for broke, that's what it was called.

She didn't have time for the Soap Opera now. What with the science fair, she had lots of schoolwork. She had to run errands for her father and Homer and make sure there was something for dinner every night. Her father still wouldn't let her touch the fry-o-lator, but she could flip burgers on the grill and knew where to rap the big black vent if the fan started rattling too much. One day Megan persuaded her babysitter to drive by, and Mo showed her all around. Megan promised to come to the grand opening, whenever that was.

A few nights later, the Wrens and Homer sat in a booth eating supper. The ball game was on TV. The front door stood propped open, letting in the breeze. Traffic honked and hummed. Dottie was musing aloud. Maybe Handsome had met a wife. Maybe when he came back, he'd bring a whole lizard family with him.

Mr. Wren slid an arm around her shoulders. He cleared his throat. "I've got an important announcement to make," he said.

They stopped eating and looked at him.

"Thanks to all your help, the time has come. We open a week from tonight."

Mo laid down her fork. Of course she'd known they'd open, someday. But hearing it for sure and definite was a jolt. Meanwhile, Dottie leaped up to perform the dance of joy.

"Can I be the waitress?" she wanted to know.

"You can be the hostess," he said. "You'll stand at the door and greet people as only you can." He looked at Homer. "It means serious butt busting. But I've got to start taking in money, or else. What do you think?"

Homer flexed his fingers as if he couldn't wait to get going. Right then, you could see the other Homer, the one Carmella described. The man who loved a challenge.

"I'm in. Now about the water pressure . . ."

While the men talked plumbing, Dottie practiced her hostessing.

"Welcome to the Wren House!" she said, sweeping her hand through the air and swishing an imaginary skirt. No one paid any attention to Mo as she stacked the dishes and carried them into the kitchen. Or when, instead of coming back to the table, she pushed open the PRIVATE door and went upstairs.

It was really going to happen. There was no turning back now. That old lump rose in her throat, and her eyes stung. Once the Wren House opened, this was where they lived. This was their home, for good.

Mo was still lying on her bed when Dottie came up. Going straight to the window, she cupped her hands around her lips, the way she did every night.

"Handsome!" she called, as if her voice could carry through the glass and out into the night. "It's almost the grand opening. You're going to miss it! Handsome Wren, can you hear me?" She waited a moment, ear to the glass, then toppled down beside Mo and pulled the covers over her head.

"K.C. says he won't come back," she said.

"K.C. gets a lot of things wrong," Mo said.

"Mommy didn't come back." The lump of covers

grew motionless. "At first I thought she would," the lump said. "But nope."

"Dottie?" Mo tried to peel back a corner of the blanket, but her sister wouldn't let her. "How come you miss Handsome so much? You only had him a little while."

The lump grew still again.

"I really want to know," Mo said. "Remember your bottles? They're still all wrapped up like mummies. And Fox Street? Where you lived your whole life? You never seem to miss it at all."

The lump wriggled.

"You want me to be sad *all* the time?" came Dottie's muffled voice.

"No! I don't want you to be sad ever. I'm just trying to understand how you do it, that's all."

Her sister dragged the blanket off her head. Squiggles of hair stuck to her cheeks.

"From you," she said.

"No. That's not how I am. Not at all."

"Because I still got you."

Dottie knuckled her cheek, and Mo knew exactly what she was going to ask. Will you always be my sister? No matter what?

But instead, Dottie held up two fingers.

"I figured it out." She wiggled one finger. "I'll never quit being your sister." She wiggled the other one. "So no matter what, you have to be mine."

"Wait a minute. Are you getting smart or something?"

"I'm way smarter than K.C." Dottie punched Mo's pillow.

Mo made her little sister go wash and brush her teeth. While she was in the bathroom, Mo looked out the window. The full moon was rising, just above the rooftops. How different it was from the sun or the stars. The moon was the one thing in the sky you felt looked back at you.

Mo listened to Dottie read aloud, and then she switched off the light. By now the moon had risen higher, shrinking to a small, bright circle. A pearl button, stitched to the sky.

Or Else

Mr. Wren hired a waitress named Daisy. Her arms were tattooed with them, as well as roses and lilies. During her interview, Daisy demonstrated how she could carry three plates at once, ranged along her muscly arms. She taught Dottie how to pour water from the side of the plastic pitcher and how to twist aluminum foil into the shape of a swan.

"I live on the other side of town," she told them. "But I want to work here. I ain't never met a boss so nice as you. And this place . . ." She cocked her head. "It reminds me of that fairy tale. The ugly duckling that became a peacock?"

Their new bartender showed up with Shawn. His name was Kelvin, and he'd been doing his wash at the Soap Opera when Carmella told him about the Wren House. Carmella had told Shawn to walk Kelvin over and introduce him.

"You're a friend of Carmella's?" Mr. Wren asked.

"Who isn't?" Kelvin had a gold earring and a good smile. "She knows I've been out of work for a while, and she told me all about your place and your great kids and . . ."

Hired.

"Shawn," called Homer from the back hall. "Give me a hand here?"

Shawn steadied the plank Homer was sawing and swept up the sawdust afterward. Homer asked if he knew how to use the claw end of a hammer and showed him a pile of boards that needed the old nails pried out. Shawn worked without stopping, as if the concentration spell had trailed him here from the Soap Opera. The next afternoon, instead of going to the Laundromat, he walked home with Mo. No sooner had he stepped inside than Homer handed him a piece of sandpaper.

WREN HOUSE GRAND OPENING. Mr. Wren put in a rush job for a real, professional sign. But before he hung it, Dottie drew a little bird inside each of the O's.

By now Mr. Wren was hardly sleeping at all. He rose at dawn, worked all day, drove Homer back to the Soap Opera or the shelter, and worked some more. His dark eyes grew more deep set. He forgot to change his clothes till Mo reminded him. Yet by some magic, he was handsomer than ever. When he left the room, a kind of phosphorescence lingered, as if he were a human glow stick.

The day before the opening, the mirror over the bar shone clear as a silver lake. Not a sticky note in sight. Her father handed Mo a sheaf of flyers and a big roll of tape.

"Plaster the neighborhood," he said. "We need to pack them in tomorrow night. Build a buzz, as they say. We're out of time, Motown. We can't even hit the ground running—we have to hit it at warp speed."

He held the door for a beer keg delivery. The guy had to dig in his heels to keep his grip on his heavy dolly.

"Wow," he said. "Is it just me, or does this place have

its own field of gravity?"

"All part of the charm," said Mr. Wren.

He let the door swing closed—then turned back to Mo. For the first time in days, or maybe weeks, he slowed down enough to truly look at her. His face got a funny expression. "Where's your hair?"

"It's called a ponytail, Daddy."

"It looks pretty. You look . . ." He fumbled for the word. "You look grown-up."

He hardly ever said things like that. Mo hugged the flyers to her chest.

"I'm not," she said. "I'm just the same."

Still he studied her, like she was a map that needed figuring out.

"You've been changing behind my back," he said.

"No," she said, clutching the flyers. "I'm still—"

"Hey," he interrupted, smiling. "That's all right. It's how life's supposed to work. Aw, Mojo! I'm sorry things have been rough. But it's all going to be worth it, I promise. Once we open, and the business takes off, you'll see. It's going to be just like I dreamed for you and Dot."

He stood back, gazing around at the yellow walls. "You were right about this paint. I keep feeling like she's here with us. But . . . not like back in the old place." His gaze rested on Mo. "Thinking of her here, I don't feel sad. I just keep remembering all the good things."

The phone rang then, and he hustled to answer.

The Truth about Corky

Mo's first stop was Al's. He sat behind his counter, reading the newspaper.

"Tomorrow's our grand opening," she said, handing him a flyer.

He scanned the paper, then handed it back to her. Rude as ever!

"Put it on my door," he said. "I'll point it out to my customers."

"Really? I mean, thanks. That's nice of you."

"It's the least I can do," he said. "I haven't been particularly neighborly. You get sick and tired of fly-by-night people." He stroked his whiskery cheek. "I was sure you'd be gone by now. Wait'll I tell Corky."

"Corky?" Mo, taping up the flyer, spun around. "You know where Corky is?"

"Nah. He still keeps that a secret. But I know one thing nobody else does." He crooked his hairy knuckle, beckoning her close. "He hit the Stellar Four. For years he bought those scratch-off lottery tickets and didn't win a nickel, then boom. Thirty-five K overnight."

It was all Mo could do not to fling the flyers like confetti.

"So Corky was lucky? He wasn't cursed after all?"

Al waggled his bushy eyebrows.

"Depends how you look at it. He owed so many people money, and he had so many friends he knew would pester him for loans, he skipped town in the middle of the night. Afterward he called me, because he had to tell someone about his big trip to Vegas." Al cracked a craggy smile. "Corky was lazy as the day is long, but he didn't waste any time gambling away all that money."

Uh-oh.

"He's as broke as ever by now. He still buys lottery tickets, though. And whenever we talk, he asks about the old place. He's still got a soft spot for it. He'll be glad to hear someone else is giving it a try."

The door opened for a woman carrying a boot split up the back. As Mo stepped outside, she heard Al telling the customer she should try the nice new restaurant opening next door.

Corky! A winner and a loser all in one. Wait till she told Shawn!

Mo taped the flyers to telephone poles and the backs of stop signs. She handed them to people on the street and slid them beneath doors. It was another beautiful day, the clouds like meringue cookies on a sky-blue baking sheet. The pigeon men were both wearing Hawaiian shirts.

A pickup truck full of furniture shot by. A bright-green armchair rode on top. Mo broke into a run, trying to see—could it be? But the truck accelerated to make the light and sped from view.

Far overhead, a plane buzzed like a silver bee. At her feet, old leaves lifted on the breeze. The whole world was in motion today. The bus shelter was empty as usual, and she watched the number eighteen zip by without stopping. For a moment Mo felt like she herself might lift off the ground and be swept away. Her father's words, *You've been changing behind my back,* echoed inside her. Sitting on the shelter bench, she leaned her head against MILO LOVES OTIS. It was peaceful in here, like always, and so warm she pulled off the blue sweatshirt and laid it on the bench beside her. By now, Mo had washed it, and the last trace of the elusive lost and found perfume was gone. By now, if the shirt smelled like anything, it was Mo herself.

Across the street, yet another sign hollered COMING SOON! Mo looked down at the single flyer left in her hand. Carmella. She wasn't coming and she wasn't going, not soon, not later. She was dependable as a bus shelter, rooted as a tree. Getting to her feet, Mo could already feel Carmella's hug, the way you can taste your favorite food just by thinking of it.

But when she got to the Soap Opera, the door was locked.

Lost and Never Found

The normally steamed-up windows were dry. Sunshine illuminated Dottie's name, hovering on the glass as if written by a ghost finger. Peering in, Mo saw that the place was empty. Something had to be very wrong. Carmella never closed.

Was she in her apartment? Mo gathered a handful of pebbles and threw them one after the other at an upstairs window. Nothing. Going back to the front door, she was just in time to see Carmella come out of her office, carrying a big book. When Mo knocked, she glanced over with a frown. But seeing who it was, Carmella crossed the room and unlocked the door. Her eyes were shadowed with a weariness that reminded Mo of her father.

"Are you sick?" asked Mo.

"No. I just need a little R & R. Or maybe some TLC." She smiled, but only with her mouth. "That sister of yours has got me talking in initials now."

"You never close," Mo insisted. "Something has to be wrong."

"Never you mind." Carmella sighed. "What's that in your hand?"

"A flyer for our grand opening tomorrow."

"Give it here." Blocking the doorway, Carmella held out her hand. "I'll hang it up."

"But who's going to see it if you're closed?"

"I'll open later, soon as I feel up to it." When Mo didn't budge, Carmella reluctantly stepped back.

Inside, the quiet was eerie. No hum of machines or chatter of customers. Even the TV was off. Mo crossed the room to the bulletin board, where Dottie's BIG REWAD notice was looking bedraggled. Mo pushed a thumbtack into her flyer, then turned to find Carmella sitting on the van seat, the book in her lap.

"Is everything ready for the opening?" Carmella asked. "Shawn and Homer have been working hard."

With a guilty twinge, Mo understood why Carmella

was acting so cold and strange.

"I'm sorry we've been hogging them," she said. "And I haven't come to visit. Homer fixed our washer, so I do the laundry at home now. It probably seems like we forgot all about you, but that's not true!"

Carmella waved her hand.

"Don't be silly, little wren. It's time those two fellows stopped hiding out here. Way past time! The Wren House is the best thing that's happened to Homer in years. He'll take on other jobs now, wait and see. And Shawn came by to brag on what a huge help he is to your daddy. Also how he plans to win a blue ribbon at the science fair. Just between you and me, you're the first person to ask him to be partners since kindergarten."

Carmella smiled, all the way this time, tiny candles lighting her eyes. "Think of all the good the Wren House has done, even before it opens! The world's going to return the love—Carmella guarantees it."

"So you're not mad at us?" Mo asked.

Carmella shook her head, but then she sighed again. "You've been on my mind, though, sugar. You and that little talk we had about curses." She patted the seat beside her. "Come here. Let me show you something."

She spread the book across their laps. It was a photo album, crammed with pictures of two girls growing up, page by page. One was tall and serious looking, the other small and always smiling. One girl's eyes were dark as plums; the other's, lit like stars. In every photo they stood or sat side by side, at a table or before a Christmas tree, in party dresses or Halloween costumes. You could just about hear someone telling them "Smile. Once more." You could feel how proud that someone was of them both.

"It's you," said Mo. "But who . . . is that your cousin?"

"That's my sister."

A black wind swept through Mo. Carmella had tricked her? But why? Why lie about wanting a sister when she had one?

When Mo raised her eyes, she understood. Carmella's face was etched with grief. Her sister—her sister must have . . . The million wishes she'd tossed into wishing wells or whispered to the stars—they'd all been wishes that her sister was still alive.

"Look," said Carmella. She paged back through the album, touching one photo after another. "See the space between us? That gap? Always there."

Mo saw it, a skinny canyon keeping them separate.

"We never got along. Ever. She was terrible shy, and

I was always a show-off. She was a good student, and I was always in trouble. It was like we existed to make each other miserable. We fought like crazy, night and day, even when we got older. After a while, we didn't know what we were fighting over anymore, but neither of us could quit hurting the other one. It broke our mother's heart. Mama was always trying to patch things up, but it didn't do any good. She used to tell us that when we were grown, we'd find each other. She said she was just living for the day we made peace and began to appreciate each other."

It was so quiet, Mo could hear Carmella swallow. She could hear the sound of her own breathing.

"But Mama died. One snowy night, she and my father were in an accident. They lived for a few days after, but then he died, and a few hours later, so did she."

"Your sister? Did she die then, too?"

Carmella pulled in her chin and leveled a look at Mo. "My sister's not dead, Mo. She lives across the river."

Mo let her head fall back against the seat. Relief, bewilderment, and something like anger whirled around inside her as if she were a blender.

"You'd think losing our parents would finally bring

us close." Carmella touched a photo, tracing the space between her and her sister. "Instead, it made things much worse. We even fought there in the hospital. Neither one of us knew how to comfort the other, and that hurt so bad, we finally just stopped speaking. Contessa lives half an hour away, but it might as well be the moon. I only hope . . . I hope Mama can't look down and see us."

Mo's emotions whirled faster yet.

"Your sister's not dead," she said. "That means . . . that means it's not too late."

Carmella closed the album. She ran her hand over the cover. Someone tried the front door but gave up and walked away.

"I wish you were right, little wren. But Contessa told me in no uncertain words—she's happier with me out of her life. We're lost to each other. Lost and not about to be found."

Inside Mo, the relief and confusion settled, but the anger kept on spinning.

"You're wrong!" she cried, and Carmella jumped as if she'd been pinched. "It doesn't have to be like that!"

"Sugar! You're too young. You can't understand."

"Yes. I can. When my mother . . . when she died,

everyone on Fox Street was so upset, they were all so sad, Dottie couldn't stand it. She wanted to cheer people up. 'Don't worry,' she told everybody. 'Our mother's only a little bit dead.' Like dying was the same as getting strep throat or . . . or having your tail break off. Like it was something that would get better, if you were just patient. She didn't understand, not for a long time."

Carmella tried to put an arm around her, but now it was Mo's turn to pull away.

"Only it's not! Dying's for good! You can't do anything about it!"

Mo stopped. Her words hung on the air, like an announcement over a speaker. They echoed inside her, and sudden tears stung her eyes. Carmella was giving her a worried look, so Mo rubbed her eyes and plunged on.

"But you . . . you could fix things with your sister. You could get her back!"

Carmella shook her head, and it was like she shook all the light out of her eyes.

"I'd never let my sister get lost from me!" Mo cried. "I mean, I might, but I'd always find her again. Always."

Carmella crossed the room and opened the door.

By now Mo felt limp as a T-shirt fresh out of the washer. How could it be? For all the people Carmella had made happy, she couldn't do it for her own self.

"She'll always be your sister," Mo said. "She can act like she's not, but she is. No matter what."

Bitterness twisted all the beauty from Carmella's face.

"I don't mean to hurt your feelings," Mo said.

"I know. You go on home now."

When Mo stepped onto the sidewalk, she heard the door lock behind her.

Outside, the day had turned strange, warm in the middle but chilly on the edges, like a puddle starting to freeze. All those fleecy clouds had knit themselves together, blocking out the sun. Mo shivered. And then she remembered.

Her sweatshirt! She'd left it in the bus shelter. Breaking into a run, Mo urged her legs past the hardware, then the Robin's Egg. She dodged a woman walking four dogs at once; she turned the corner and ran past the Pit Stop. The park was in sight now, the shelter just visible through the screen of new leaves. The number eighteen was pulling up. A passenger stepped out of the shelter.

Let it still be there! Don't let them take it! In Mo's head, the blue sweatshirt tumbled around, tangling with a pair of fuzzy yellow sleeves, knotting together. Blue and yellow, blue and yellow, they spun, the pearly buttons of the sweater surfacing and sinking.

The passenger jumped aboard, and just as Mo ran up, the bus pulled away. She stood panting, trying not to breathe in the cloud of exhaust, afraid to look.

As always, the orange plastic bench was empty. No person. No sweatshirt.

Mo scoured the park, searching everywhere, in case someone had picked it up and dropped it. Under bushes, beside the swings. But it was no use.

Peeled, that was how she felt. Like she'd lost some protective layer. First Carmella and then her favorite shirt, the two most comforting things in her life. She'd lost them both.

The wind shook the trees, and Mo's bare arms grew goose bumps. The anger she'd felt at Carmella died away, leaving behind regret. If only she'd found gentler, more helpful words, the way Carmella herself would have done! Mo had missed her chance to boomerang all that kindness.

She rubbed her arms. A human being could feel

peeled, just like a grape. She took one more turn around the park and then slowly walked home. Everywhere she looked, flyers for the Grand Opening rippled in the rising wind.

The Curse, Part Four

The next day, the day of the opening, the sky was still overcast and the air had a mean, untrustworthy feel. Up in her nest, the sparrow hunkered down. Mo hoped her babies wouldn't hatch yet. It was no day to be small and featherless.

With all his jobs done, Homer asked Mo if anything upstairs needed fixing. Carrying his toolbox, he followed her to her bedroom and examined her window. Pulling out a can, he sprayed all around the frame, then whittled away the old paint with a knife. At last he gave Mo the nod.

"Let 'er rip," he said.

Bending her knees, she pushed. The window didn't want to let go—nothing in this place could ever surrender without a big fuss!

"Try again," said Homer. "Grunt this time."

"Grrr . . . unt!" Mo felt it giving way, gradually then all at once. Hallelujah! The window defied gravity and rocketed up. Fresh air rushed in for the first time in years. You could just about hear the room taking deep gulps of it.

"It's getting cold out there," said Homer, repacking his tools. "Better close it."

But not yet. Mo stretched her arms out. The sidewalk tree was so close. If it grew a little fatter, and her arms a little longer, she'd be able to touch it.

The phone jangled. It was Mercedes.

"Tonight?" she said when she heard the news. "I wish I was there!"

"Me too," said Mo.

Mo carried the phone downstairs, where all the lights were on. Their brightness made the dining-room walls look paler, more than ever like moonbeams. Behind the bar, the glasses twinkled like a tiny galaxy. Mo stood back, surveying their work. If you thought of the glossy green floor as Earth, they'd created their own little tilting planet, complete with moon and stars.

"Everything's ready," Mo said.

They'd set the tables with the new silverware. Inside every water glass, Mo had tucked a napkin folded into a fan, the way Daisy had taught her. Her father was in the kitchen, singing as he sliced onions. Even though Mo still didn't like meat loaf, its baking made the air smell homey. Pretty soon Daisy and Kelvin the bartender would report for duty.

"It's not snowing, is it?" asked Mercedes.

"Snowing!" Mo laughed. "In May?"

"Da always checks the Cleveland weather, and she said something about a freak blizzard."

Mo cracked the front door. Outside, the temperature had dropped some more, and the air had a hollow-eggshell feel. She shut the door quickly.

"She's at her bridge club. It's all working out, Mo! Three-C found her this really excellent physical therapist, and now she goes up and down stairs, and she sleeps in the room next to me. Monette's so much calmer now. Yesterday we got a pink sweater in the mail from Grandma Steinbott. What if it's a boy? Monette won't have the test, because Three-C wants to be surprised. Can you believe how primitive?"

The door opened and in blew Shawn, rubbing his

hands together and puffing his cheeks.

"Something's weird out there," he said.

"Who's that?" asked Mercedes.

"Just Shawn."

"Yo!" He leaned into the phone, smelling like winter. "Yo, Megan?" Mo pushed him away.

"Merce, I better go."

"Shawn who?"

"Nobody! I really have to—"

"Wait. I know it's bad timing. But you and I always swore never to keep secrets from each other."

Mo heard her best friend inhale.

"I lost my plum pit," Mercedes said.

"Your plum pit."

"I'm sorry! Maybe one of the cleaning people threw it out, I don't know. I can't find it anyplace. I was going to tell you at Da's, but I didn't. Now it's almost spring, and I keep thinking you'll call and say the time has come and let's fulfill our pact and . . ."

Mo stared at the window. By now it had grown so dark outside, all she could see was her own reflection. The plum pit. Guiltily, she realized she hadn't given it a thought since she'd visited Fox Street. She had forgotten all about it.

"I could've gotten another plum at the store. But

I'd never lie to you." Mercedes sighed. "You probably have yours in some sacred place where nothing can happen to it."

"I do. But it's okay, Merce."

"It was just a symbol, right? You never really lose the stuff you love, right? Isn't that what you told Da? It stays with you, like the moon or something? Da can't wait for you to come visit this summer, Mo. The other day we were talking about you and she said you're an excellent scout. What's that supposed to mean? Did you join Girl Scouts?"

"No. I . . ."

"Is Shawn cute? Oh, never mind, you've got to go. I really wish I could be there tonight! I'd order the Mojo!"

"Bye, Merce."

"Bye, Mo."

No sooner did she click off than the phone rang again, and this time it was Daisy, the waitress, calling from her apartment.

"Lake effect, schmake effect, this ain't natural," she said. "Crud! If only I'd bought those snow tires when I had the cash! Tell your father I'll be there soon as I can."

A steely curtain hung across the sky, letting in only

a thin crack of light along the hem. Mo could hear her father in the kitchen, belting out "All You Need Is Love."

"Shawn, it can't snow in May, can it?"

"Believe it or not," he said.

He strolled around the room, admiring the napkins and sports posters. In the new bathroom, he flushed the toilet and activated the hand dryer, proud as if he'd built the place from scratch.

"I think we did it," he said at last.

"What?"

"Busted the curse."

"Yeoww!"

A tortured yowl split the air.

The You-Know-What, Part Five

Mr. Wren was swearing like a star contestant in an inappropriate-word contest. When Mo and Shawn ran into the kitchen, he gritted his teeth but stayed bent in two, as if bowing to an audience.

"Daddy! What happened?"

He tried to straighten up but instead let out another yowl.

"Need. To. Lie. Down."

Getting him up the stairs was like climbing Mount Everest with a hundred-year-old man. Mr. Wren inched himself down onto his bed.

"Asrin," he said through clenched teeth. "Eating ad."

Dottie came running with a blanket and heating pad. Mo fetched water and ibuprofen.

"I'll . . . *yow!* . . . be okay." His eyes sank shut, then flew back open. "The meat loaves! Mo, make sure they don't burn."

"Okay. Just rest, Daddy. Don't worry."

Don't worry.

Back downstairs, Kelvin was letting himself in the back door. He stomped his feet and shook his head.

"This beats all," he said. "Where's the boss?"

"He hurt his back."

Kelvin gave the unsliced onions, unpeeled potatoes, and unwashed lettuce the once-over.

"Daisy?"

"She's going to be late."

He looked from Mo to Shawn, as alarmed as if someone had told him he had to walk to California.

"My father will be down soon." Mo pulled on two giant mitts and opened the oven door. Heat blasted her face. The meat loaves sizzled, but she couldn't tell if they were done or not. Probably it was better to overcook meat than take a chance on serving it undercooked. Hadn't one of the old owners served bad meat and made people sick? Though when it came to burgers, her father said a touch of pinkness was essential. She slammed the oven.

"Bad luck comes in threes," Kelvin said. "We've got the storm, your father, and Daisy. Things should start looking up any minute." With a dubious smile, he went into the dining room.

Dottie came in wearing the only dress she owned. She must have grown since last time she'd put it on, because Mo could see how it pinched her armpits and bit her waist. Dottie had squeezed into it anyway, so she could be a proper hostess.

"Daddy doesn't look so good. His face is like this." She pulled her eyes down at the corners and gritted her teeth.

The wind whistled around the corner of the building. Through the window, they saw the snow beginning to fall.

"Check it out!" Shawn's voice was hushed. In slow motion, like Handsome on the hunt, he extended his wrist. "It stopped," he said. "Time has stopped all over the world."

The three of them stared at the petrified face of his beloved watch. Dottie gave it a tap. Nothing.

"The you-know-what," he whispered. "It's back."

Dottie grabbed Mo's oven mitts and pressed them to her ears. "I can't hear you!" she shouted. "La la la!" She spun around, knocking into a big bag of potatoes and sending them rolling across the floor.

"Hey!" Mo grabbed her arm. "I need you to help, not make trouble!"

"Let's use indoor voices." Dottie smoothed her too-short skirt. "And remember, there is no I in 'team.'" Picking up a potato peeler, she asked Shawn, "How does this thing work?"

In the dining room, Kelvin was setting up the bar. On TV, the weather lady warned motorists to stay off the roads until midnight. Mo hurried out into the hall and pushed through the PRIVATE door.

Upstairs, Mr. Wren hadn't moved. His face was the color of ashes.

"All the time I worked for the flippin' water department, my back never gave out!"

Mo had never seen her father like this. Angry, frustrated, in a rotten mood, his thumb whacked or his hand burned—but never like this. He'd been cut down, the earth gone right out from under him.

"Get me that extra-strength stuff," he told her, and when Mo brought the medicine, he gulped a couple of tablets. Gripping Mo's arm, he tried to swing his legs onto the floor but fell back against the cushions.

"Not going to happen," he said.

He hadn't switched on a lamp, and the room was dark and chilly. Mo pushed up the thermostat. Fat, airy flakes filled the window. It was the kind of snow that made you think of ballerinas in white tutus—bits of lace, downy feathers. As they pressed against the glass, Mo could see each flake's starry little points, its intricate beauty. Beauty—talk about stubborn things.

When she turned back from the window, her father's face was the face of someone waving good-bye, trying to keep the place he was leaving behind in sight as long as possible.

"I can't cook. Go downstairs," he said. "Put the CLOSED sign up."

Mo thought of her flyers, flapping in the wind all over the neighborhood. What if they couldn't open for days? All the expensive fresh food they'd bought would go bad. Their customers would find other places to eat.

Mo feared if she sat on the bed it might hurt him, so she knelt down instead. A cold draft swept across the floor. They were out of money. It was now or never. Her father turned his face away, as if the sight of her made him feel worse.

"This isn't how things were supposed to go," he said.

"I know! You never get hurt! You're strong!" The floor was so cold. Mo trembled, her eyes filling with tears. "You're the strongest person in the world! It's the curse! It has to be!"

"Not that again."

"You worked so hard! You gave it your heart and soul and all our money too! You did so much good stuff, but only bad's coming back!"

Mo was never going to stop shivering. Putting her arms around herself didn't help at all. The cold was too deep inside her.

"No curse did this to me, Mo," her father said. "Unless working harder than you ever knew you could, unless that's a curse." His voice grew stronger with every word. "Or chasing a dream with everything you've got, and then some, unless that's a curse."

Outside, the snow made a ghostly, whooshing sound.

"You're shivering," he said. "Where's your sweatshirt?"

"I don't know."

He turned his face away again. Defeat hovered, cloudlike, over his head. Careful not to jostle him,

Mo plumped his pillow and smoothed his blanket.

"Do as I say." He closed his eyes. "Tell Kelvin and Daisy to be careful driving home, and I'll make it up to them for coming in. Make sure your sister gets something to eat."

"But—"

"Go on. I need you to be my partner. You can handle this. I'm trusting you."

The hallway was graveyard cold. Her window—she'd left it open! The sill and floor were dusted white. When Mo yanked it shut, the flakes spattered against the glass, angry they couldn't get in.

Mo sat on her bed. So what? she tried to tell herself. So what if we can't open? So what if the Wren House is a failure, just like all those other businesses? Did she really want to live here anyway? This street without a real name? This stubborn old place, that skinny sidewalk tree, a school full of unfamiliar kids? Some of them really nice? And neighbors who wished you well, and a woman with eyes like candles, who just the thought of her made you happy and sad, both at once? So what, so what, so . . .

Mo pulled her blanket over her head. Underneath, it was itchy and dark. Nothing at all like nestling inside the yellow sweater, cradled in moonbeams, sheltered and loved. That was lost. Lost lost lost, for good.

"Mo." The corner of the blanket lifted. "Come out."

"No."

But Dottie inched the blanket higher, and Mo didn't try to stop her. Up the blanket rose, like a stage curtain. There was Dottie's chin. Her nose. Her eyes. A potato peel stuck in her wild red hair.

"There," Dottie said. "There you are."

She scratched her stomach through her too-tight dress. And then she climbed into Mo's lap. Toasty as she was, it was like having a giant baked potato nestle against you. The warmth rolled off her, making its way inside Mo, spreading, glowing.

"Daddy can't get up," said Mo.

"So it's just you and me? My my my." Dottie pondered for a moment, then jumped off the bed. "You need to brush your hair, Mo. Waitresses have to look neat." And then she was down the stairs.

Slowly Mo climbed off the bed. Picking up the brush, she discovered her hair was long enough to tuck the end in and make a bun. Stepping into the hallway, she paused to listen outside her father's door. *Putt putt putt.* That was the sound of his snore, like a small boat making its way through deep waves. The medicine had helped him sleep. Good.

Trying not to think, Mo started for the stairs, but halfway down, her brain got the best of her. She stopped, resting a hand on the wall crazy with cracks. What did she think she was doing? Just because Dottie didn't question that they'd open. Just because their father had worked harder at this than at anything else in his whole life. Just because the rest of her family was so brave, so hopeful, did that mean that she . . .

Her feet were moving. The rest of Mo nearly tripped trying to keep up with them. She pushed open the PRIVATE door just in time to watch Dottie perform a deep curtsy for their very first customers.

"Welcome to the Wren House. Enjoy your dining experience!"

"Why, thank you," said Sarah. She set Min down on the floor and looked up. Her rosy face dimpled. "Look, Min! It's Mo!"

The Grand(?) Opening

Stiff armed, the baby sped forward. But the room's slope was too much for her short legs, and she toppled backward, landing on her bottom. Grabbing the leg of a chair, she shook it and laughed uproariously.

"Tch tch." Dottie smoothed the skirt of her hostess dress. "That baby is wild."

"We called the other day." Tim set Min back on her feet and wrestled her out of her jacket. "Your dad told us about the opening. We were afraid our old beater wouldn't make it through the weather, so we took the number eighteen. We loved the bus, huh, Min?"

"Round and round," she sang.

Dottie clucked her tongue, then hurried to greet their next customers, who turned out to be Shawn's mother and sister. They both had lively hair and inquisitive faces, just like Shawn, and they looked around with approval.

"I could tell you were cute," the sister told Mo, "from how shy Shawn acts when he says your name."

"And he says it a dozen times day," his mother put in. Under her coat she still wore her nurse's uniform. "Thanks for letting him make himself at home here, Mo. My friend Carmella told me what good folks you all are."

"Where is that bro anyway?" asked the sister.

"Yo!" On cue he dashed out of the kitchen, waving a spatula, wrapped in an apron that went around him three times.

"Good thing you're not cooking for real!" His sister gave a hoot. "I'm not spending my night in the emergency room!"

"Ha ha," said Mo. "Ha ha ha."

"What can I get you ladies to drink?" Kelvin called from behind the bar. "All drinks are on the house tonight, isn't that so, Ms. Wren?" He jerked his head toward the kitchen, and said in a low voice, "Do I smell something burning?"

Mo ran. Tugging the oven door open, she found the meat loaves transformed into smoking bricks.

"This is serious!" she cried. "People are coming! We have to feed them!"

"Mashed potatoes." Shawn was carving potatoes into strange, blobby shapes. "Everyone loves mashed potatoes."

In the refrigerator she found her father's special burgers, seasoned and ready to grill. She could do that. The fry-o-lator—that she'd never tried. The oil got so hot, it popped.

Dottie darted in, flouncing her hostess skirt. "Your friend Megan and her family are here! Min spilled her milk. Your sister's not ugly, Shawn! Sarah says can they have some bread or something. Uh-oh—I hear the door!" She ran back out, skirt flying.

"Maybe we can scrape these meat loaves," said Shawn. "Like when you burn the toast."

Mo tore open a big bag of rolls, filled some baskets, and carried them out to the dining room. The front door kept on opening. People stamped their feet, brushed the snow from their heads, and looked around with pleasure, as if a nice neighborhood restaurant was just what they needed on a night like this. Dottie introduced the shaved-head guy from

Pet Universe; and here came the old couple who ran the Pit Stop, and a distinguished-looking man she'd never seen before, accompanied by—could it be? Gilda, the actress from the Soap Opera, a little tiara of snowflakes glittering in her hair.

"Look!" cried Dottie, waving her arms. "It's a real restaurant!"

Except that nobody had any food.

As Mo set the bread on tables, people began giving her orders. Kelvin, handing out drinks all around, pushed a pen and pad into her hands.

"Daisy just called. She's not going to make it. It's me and you, sink or swim!"

"Mo!" Megan was waving. "Come meet my parents. I made them come, even though the roads are extremely treacherous."

"I'd like the cheese omelet with extra cheese."

"The Mojo, well done. Not rare, not medium. *Well done.*"

"Can I get both fries and mashed potatoes with my meat loaf?"

"Mo! Your hair looks so cute in a bun!"

"Pierre and I had reservations for the Elegant Persimmon." Since last Mo had seen her, Gilda had dyed her white-blond hair midnight black. "But Carmella swore if I didn't come here instead, she'd shrink all my clothes!"

"Two dry martinis," said Pierre. "And an order of *pommes frites*."

"That's French for fries," said Gilda.

"All right! Sure! Coming right up!" Mo wrote it down and wheeled back to the room. Hungry mouths were everywhere. From every side, people fixed her with ravenous looks. What had she been thinking? She hadn't been thinking, that was the problem. She'd been wishing, and now look! This was worse than closing down. She'd made things much worse. Who'd ever come back here after tonight? At least her father couldn't see what was happening. All these customers who'd made their way through the weather would go home hungry and disappointed, the very opposite of his dream.

"Could we have some more water, at least?"

"How about butter? Could I at least have some butter?"

Min toddled over and flung her arms around Mo's knees. Outside, a harsh sound, like the surface of the world being scraped away, started up. Shawn poked his head out of the kitchen, took one look, and dove back inside. It was hopeless.

Sarah picked up Min. Her usually dimply face was full of concern.

"Mo? Is everything okay? Where's your father?"

"He . . . he hurt his back."

"Oh, my goodness. Badly?"

"He . . . well . . . yeah. It's bad."

Sarah and Tim looked as upset as if one of them had gotten hurt.

"He can't cook?" Sarah's hands flew to her cheeks. "There's nobody in the kitchen? With this crowd?"

A look darted between Sarah and Tim. "Let's get out of here," no doubt. They both nodded.

But instead of the door, Sarah headed for the kitchen.

"Bye-bye, Mama," called Min.

"What's she doing?" Mo stared at Tim.

"Sarah's had a million jobs, including short-order cook in a diner," he said as Min draped a napkin over his head. "She's great," he said from under it. "Don't you worry."

The Craziest Thing

Some moments in your life stand out clear and sharp as something snipped with brand-new scissors. Others blur, like the view from the Tilt-A-Whirl. Those moments are nothing but color and light, the edges of one thing melting another.

Tonight had both kinds of moments.

Within minutes of Sarah disappearing into the kitchen, Shawn rushed out and thrust two burger platters at Mo.

"This one's rare, this one's medium."

Thus commenced the blurry, Tilt-A-Whirl portion of the night.

Menus, water, drinks, bread. Dishes, dirty dishes, wipe that table. More ketchup coming right up. The meat loaf is unavailable tonight, but please enjoy a complimentary salad instead. Shooed out of the kitchen, Shawn moved so fast, he might have been on Rollerblades. His talent for being everywhere at once had never come in handier. Dottie seated the pigeon men and their wives at a window table. Four orders of Dottie's Delight, hold the meatballs. They were all veginarians, she explained. Kelvin ran the cash register, helping Mo make change.

"Where is Carmella, anyway?" asked Gilda when Mo served their onion rings. "I thought for sure she'd be here! Something must have happened."

Mo's heart gave a twist. In spite of yesterday, she'd hoped Carmella would come. But as the night sped by, Carmella was the one person who didn't appear.

At last customers stopped coming in, but those already there lingered, reluctant to go back out into the night. Homer—when had he gotten here?—made a trip to the Robin's Egg, where he bought out all the day's leftover sweets. Dottie served sugar cookies and fruit tarts all around. The scraping sound stopped and in came Al, wearing his big rubber galoshes. He leaned his snow shovel in a corner, and Kelvin served him something called a hot toddy, which made Al very cheerful.

"Au revoir!" called Gilda, throwing kisses.

Tim sat pinned in a booth, Min asleep on one side of him and Dottie on the other. Shawn and his family pulled on their coats.

"Thanks, Shawn," said Mo. "We couldn't have done it without you."

"Look." He held out his wrist. His watch had started back up again, just as strangely as it had stopped. "All the times are wrong," he said. "But I can fix that."

"He's a good boy," his mother told Mo. "Not everybody sees that, but he is." She tapped him on the head. "Where's your new hat? Don't tell me!"

"Tonight was off the hook," Kelvin said. He gave the bar one last swipe. "Can't wait to see what tomorrow's like!"

Tomorrow. There'd be a tomorrow, after all.

At last Sarah came out of the kitchen, folding up her apron.

"I left you a colossal mess," she apologized. "But I'm afraid if we don't get going, we'll miss the last bus."

"Thank you," said Mo. "I mean, that doesn't even cover it. You saved us!"

Tim pulled Sarah tight. They touched foreheads.

Mo could just imagine them doing that in the kitchen on Fox Street, while Min banged the pots and pans. She could see them sitting by the window, looking out at the plum tree.

"We always hoped to get the chance to pay your dad back." Tim was trying to fit Min into her jacket, but, sound asleep, she flopped around like a doll. "At least a little."

"You don't need to pay us back," Mo said. "You already paid us."

Min's hat was violently pink and handmade—old Mrs. Steinbott's work, for sure. Sarah pulled it over Min's shiny black hair and tied it under her chin.

"We still can't believe he sold it to us instead of that other couple. They bid so much higher." Sarah hoisted the lolling baby onto her shoulder. "We could never have matched them. No bank was ever going to loan us that kind of money."

She stroked Min's cheek, and the baby's eyelashes fluttered. Mo's brain had a little flutter of its own.

"Excuse me," she said. "What'd you just say?"

"When he called to say he wanted us to have your house—it was just the craziest thing anybody ever did. He said he knew we'd take good care of the place, and be happy there, and that was what mattered most to you Wrens." Sarah tightened her arms around Min. "Not a day goes by we don't feel grateful."

"They say you don't just find a home. You make one." Tim smiled and looked around. "Looks like you're doing a good job of that yourselves."

"Tell your dad we'll be back soon," said Sarah. "I'm dying to taste his version of the Mojo. Tell him we plan to be your star customers, okay?"

The sidewalk out front was shoveled clean. Overhead, wisps of cloud played tag across the black sky. The first star was so low in the sky, it looked like a diamond barrette clipped to the branches of the sidewalk tree. Mo waved as the little family walked toward the bus shelter.

There'd never been enough money. That's why he'd cut corners, and done everything himself, and struggled on, even as the money and his back gave out. And all this time, he hadn't told her, because he didn't want her to worry. Stubborn as he was, he'd stuck to his dream to make her and Dottie feel as safe and loved as if they were wrapped in moonbeams.

The world was bright and sharp, its edges snipped with quick, silver scissors.

Daddy. Mo pushed open the door.

The Right People

Dottie was still asleep, curled up like a seashell. Dirty glasses and plates littered some tables, and the floor was a mess of crumbs and slushy footprints. Rushing past the mirror behind the bar, Mo saw how, with her hair piled up, her cheekbones stuck out in a new and unfamiliar way. It looked as if she'd been snipped sharp and fresh too.

She shoved open the PRIVATE door and there he was, sitting on the steps.

"I made it halfway." He rubbed the side of his face. His eyes were groggy, his beautiful curls matted to his head. "That's progress."

Mo climbed up to sit beside him.

"I overdid it on the pain meds. It was like I got hit by a two-by-four. I had some whacked-out dreams!" He sniffed the air, then cautiously turned his head. "You and your sister got something to eat?"

"Umm, we didn't have time." She leaned against him, testing him out. When he didn't flinch or yowl, she went on, "We were too busy serving everybody else."

Her father nodded, still too stupefied to process much. He rubbed his face some more and then his knee, trying to wake himself up.

"People came, Daddy. Just like you dreamed. I mean, like you dreamed for real. Sarah and Tim were the first ones here. She can cook. Not as good as you, but people seemed happy."

Mr. Wren pinched the bridge of his nose and squeezed his eyes shut.

"Wait. What? People were here?"

"Lots of people, Daddy. The buzz is on!"

Like someone in a fairy tale who thinks he's been asleep for a night, only to discover a hundred years have gone by, her father's mouth dropped.

"You opened?" He gaped. "On your own?"

"No, not on our own. With lots of help." She touched

his cheek. "They told me, Daddy. About you selling our house to them instead of the rich people."

At last Mo saw the fog lift from his eyes.

"Sarah said it was the kindest thing anyone ever did, and they can't ever repay you. But they did tonight." Mo grabbed his Band-Aided hand. "They saved us, Daddy."

"What do you know." Mr. Wren sandwiched her hand in his. "What do you know."

"Daddy, you picked the right people. I'm glad you sold them our house."

"Mojo."

The two of them leaned against each other, making the stair creak. Her arms and legs were beginning to let her know how hard they'd worked tonight. His sandpapery hands held hers tight. Here they were, here they were. In this world full of things that traveled—people, buses, sweaters—here they were, a fixed point, like a star, or a tree, or a bus shelter. The rest of the world rushed right by, while they held fast.

The door at the bottom of the steps opened. Dottie, her hostess dress streaked with something gross, her cheek rumpled with sleep, climbed up and wedged herself between Mo and the wall. Narrow as it was, that step somehow stretched to let her in, like every other place in the world.

"Are you all right now, Daddy?" she asked.

"I don't know. But I guess I better be." His arm worked its way up and around them both. "Somehow I woke up with a business to run."

"Hostessing is way harder than it looks." Dottie yawned. "But I'm good at it."

That was turning out to be true of more things than Mo had ever dreamed.

Stumpy

Snow was one of those things that didn't really go away but only turned into something else. Something like a drink for baby birds. When Mo stood beneath the sidewalk tree the next morning, she heard them up there, cheeping for all they were worth. She ran back inside to get some bread crusts, and by the time she came back out, someone had scattered seed beneath the tree.

Next door, Al knocked on his window and gave a hairy thumbs-up.

Melting snow gurgled in the gutters. It slipped from the tree branches to the sidewalk in wild, exploding clumps. Overhead, the sun did a victory dance, having defeated winter for good.

"What do you think?" called a voice.

Mo squinted against the glare. A table was walking toward her.

"Sidewalk dining! People love it. And look, there's just enough room."

No sooner did Carmella set down the round plastic table than a sparrow lighted on it, cocking its head to ask, "Where's my menu?"

"Carmella!" Mo was so glad to see her. It had been three days, since the afternoon before the opening. Carmella wore a church dress and good shoes, and she carried a purse and a shopping bag.

"One of my customers is moving and asked if she could swap some lawn furniture for a bunch of free loads. I have four chairs too." She fumbled with her purse strap, nervous for the first time in memory. The light in her eyes leaped up, disappeared, and leaped up again, as if her own personal wiring was about to short out.

"I'm going to see her."

She could only mean one person.

"Contessa?"

Carmella nodded.

"For real? You two made up?"

"No no no." Carmella waved a hand in front of her face. "I haven't even talked to her. I've called and called, but she recognizes my number and won't pick up."

"But . . . you're still going there?"

"That lecture you gave me, about if your sister's lost, you find her. You just find her! I couldn't get it out of my head. And then along came that freak snowstorm. It was just like the night our parents . . . well." She waved that hand again. "I have to try."

The sparrow did a loop-de-loop over their heads, above the tree, beyond the roof.

Carmella twisted her purse strap and threw a look in the direction of the park.

"Even if she turns me away, I have to try."

Mo's heart jittered. What if Contessa wouldn't open her door? What if she let Carmella knock and knock till she finally gave up and went away again? Carmella was risking getting her heart broken, once and for all.

"You're really brave," Mo said.

"Say it again," said Carmella.

"You're . . ."

"Oh, sugar." Carmella grabbed her hands. "I'll repeat that to myself all the way there. If she turns me away . . . and even if she lets me in, after all these years . . . pain doesn't heal so quick when you're our age. But I have to try! Oh, did I say that already?" Carmella wrapped Mo in a suffocating hug. "I've got to catch the number twenty-three. It's due any minute. Wish me luck." She started down the street but whirled around and flew back. "I didn't even ask how your daddy is! Homer told me . . ."

"He's much better. Hurry, or you'll miss the bus. I'll be here when you get back."

"Oh, don't I know it, little wren!" She started off again but ran back one more time. "I almost forgot. This is for you and Red. It's that time of year."

She thrust the shopping bag at Mo and hurried down the street. You could practically see happiness and love floating just ahead of her, in sight, almost in reach. Go, thought Mo. Go, Carmella!

Here came that sparrow arrowing back to the tree. It was one of those days when, late afternoon, the sun and the moon share the sky. The moon was faint and low, patiently waiting its turn to shine. It was a lopsided moon, but look again and you'd see the missing piece, there and not there, both at once.

Mo set the shopping bag on the table and pulled out a pair of gardening gloves. Both thumbs were stained the color of grass. These gloves were well acquainted with growing things. And look, Carmella had put in packets of seed, too. Big-headed zinnias, curly-leafed parsley, a variety of pea called Little Marvel. They still had the price stickers on and couldn't be from the lost and found. This time, Carmella had given Mo and Dottie something brand-new.

Though, if you thought about it—if you were a thinker—seeds went round and round, too. Seeds . . .

"Mo." The front door opened a crack, and Dottie's head poked out. Her voice was hushed. "Come here."

Inside, Dottie held out her arms as if offering a bouquet. Her eyes were round as marbles. For the second time in minutes, Mo's heart began to beat too fast.

"Dottie? What happened? Are you okay?"

Her little sister didn't speak. Instead, slowly and gently, like a bud spreading its petals, she parted her hands.

Up popped a pointy, spotted head.

"No. Is it?" Mo leaned close. "It is. Oh, Handsome!" she breathed. "Handsome Wren."

He shot out his tongue, then ducked back inside.

"How? Where? I can't believe it!"

"I was watching TV and saw something move and looked and it was him. Just sitting there, staring at the

TV with me! Just like we used to do!" Dottie lifted her hands to her face and spoke into her fingers. "You came back. You missed your home and you came back. I knew you would! I always knew!"

"What's going on?" Mr. Wren, still moving as if the surface of the earth was more treacherous than people guessed, came in from the kitchen. "Nah!" he said, when Dottie showed him. "It can't be."

Where had Handsome been all this time? How had he survived? Down the basement maybe, hunting spiders and thousand leggers and huddling near the boiler for warmth. Or was Dottie right, and he'd had his wild adventure but come back, homesick for them?

"Is he all right?" Mo asked.

"Look." Dottie parted her hands, revealing Handsome's backside. Where once he'd had a magnificent tail, there was now a hideous bulge.

"Ooh," said Mo. "Ooh wee."

"But it looks like it's healing okay," said Mr. Wren. "And look at that—I bet that's a new tail growing in."

"I know. Isn't he so smart? You deserve a new name," Dottie told him. "Stumpy, that's what I'm going to call you now. Handsome Stumpy Wren."

"Welcome back, H.S.W."

Mo carried his tank from the kitchen, where they'd stored it, and set it on a table. Dottie plugged in the heat rock, and when they put him inside, Handsome hopped right on. He struck a noble, dignified pose, as if waiting to be photographed for *Ripley's.* World's Most Astonishing Lizard.

"We have to go buy him crickets," Dottie said. "But first I have to make him a present." She found paper and her crayons and got to work.

"Hey," said Mr. Wren, pointing out the window. "What's that table doing there?"

"For outdoor dining," said Mo. "And Daddy, maybe we should plant some vegetables. We could put 'garden fresh' on the menu."

"The backyard's nothing but sun and dirt. It's made for growing things."

Mo pulled on the gardening gloves. Who knew where else they'd been? What other gardens they'd planted and tended? At the table, Dottie was working so hard, her crayon snapped in two. All around them, the yellow walls caught and held the new spring light. Mo flexed her gloved fingers. Probably the most important thing wasn't to think about what you'd lost but what you'd found. Here they were, all three—all four—of them together.

"Ta da!" Dottie held up her sign.

What do you know. By now, Dottie Wren had learned how to spell something completely, perfectly right.

HOME SWEET HOME.

Acknowledgments

Thanks to my incomparable agent, Sarah Davies, who continues to show me what I can do. Gratitude to my superb editor, Donna Bray, who gently steers me home when I get lost. Bouquets to all the kind, supportive librarians, teachers, booksellers, bloggers, and fellow writers who daily teach me what a wonderful community I've joined. All my love to Paul, who sustains me with encouragement and spicy food. And to my darling muses, Zoe, Phoebe, and Delia—who and where would I be without you? Every day you help me understand how lucky I am.